GARNET FIRE

To Brenna,
I hope you find your
magic!

Ana Michelle

GEMSTONE WITCH SERIES
ANA MICHELLE
BOOK 1

For Mike England and Ann Grenier. I miss you both and wish you were here to witness this.

CONTENTS

PROLOGUE

THE BIRDS' MORNING SONG was the only noise to be heard in the predawn light of the otherwise silent streets. A piercing scream echoed across the frozen ground, shattering the calm night. Doors flung open and people flooded out onto the dirt roads still in their dressing gowns. Households huddled together to maintain their warmth. Husbands standing in front of their family, as if to shield them from the scene unfolding on the street.

"Witch!" A shrill female voice rang out. An accusing finger pointing at a dark-skinned figure now sprawled in the middle of the street, "She's a witch! She cursed me!" the woman sobbed, her shoulders hunching as she curled over herself. Her husband pulled her trembling form against him. As the town watched two men stepped forward, away from their families, to lift the pleading slave girl from the street.

"Please, I did no such thing," The slaves voice trembled, eyes pleading for anyone to believe her.

"Take her to the magistrate," the women's husband demanded. The two men nodded before dragging her off to the town magistrate's home. Her sobs and pleas floated back to the townspeople.

There in the still nearly dark street, the members of fourteen families all looked at each other with understanding in their eyes. Their worst fear had just come true. A witch hunt was starting in Salem. They went back into their houses, tucking their children back into their beds. Then they sat with their spouses in the rising light and quietly spoke of their fears. They knew that life as they knew it, had just changed forever.

After that first accusation there were more every week. So many accusations that no one could keep up with who had been accused and who had not. Everyone was on edge, not knowing who would be taken away next as an accused witch. The town witches did their best to stay calm and keep their heads down. They stopped spending time together to keep suspicion down. They limited their meetings to only the weekly mass. No longer did they gather in the woods or under the moonlight, instead they whispered their spells in dark of night, hiding in the shelter of their homes. The only thing they could be sure of was that none of the accused were actual witches. At least not in the beginning. Then the fateful day came, a true witch was arrested in Salem.

It was five months after that first frightful scream of "witch." The witches gathered with the rest of Salem and watched as Bridget Bishop was led to the gallows. The townspeople jeered as she was led to the executioner. Bridget stood, head bowed as the hangman slipped his noose around her neck then the feet of their sister witch swung from the gallows. Her last breaths were harsh gasps that filled the air. The witches' eyes met, this time in true fear and terror, as the crowd around them cheered. Things in Salem were getting very dangerous for those born to magic, and those who loved them. They were now to be the enemies of those they had once called friend and neighbor.

Soon small notes were being passed from hand to hand at weekly mass during greetings or smuggled in baskets of produce at the market. As hysteria began to spread through the streets of Salem, hopeless panic settled over the witches. They knew they must protect themselves or join their sister in death. Thus, they began working to form a plan to protect themselves and all their future descendants.

Each of the remaining thirteen families agreed to lock their powers into precious gems which they would then fasten into thirteen different magical objects. The gems would hold the most powerful of their magical abilities until released. With the gained sense of security they would retain the power they harnessed from nature around them. They would then hide the enchanted objects in a protected and blessed clearing in the woods a day's walk from the village. Three days before the agreed upon night, one of the remaining thirteen witches was accused of witchcraft and taken to the magistrate as had quickly become custom. With a grim nod, the rest agreed to continue with the plans that they had decided on. They would be losing an ability, but they could not risk waiting any longer.

Over the next two days each family traveled from Salem, giving different reasons they needed to travel to other nearby towns. They set off in different directions as to not rouse the towns suspicion while tension was high, and townspeople were looking for odd behavior.

As the silver moon rose full over the woods, they met. The remaining twelve families arrived at the clearing, objects in hand. The first object placed was a square table to act as the Altar in the very heart of the clearing. The table was a little less than an arms width and had seven red garnet gems inlaid into the wood in the center, one gem at each point of a seven-point star. One by one the matriarchal witch from each family stepped forward and placed an item on the Altar, leaving a space for the missing item from the arrested member in hopes that one day it could be added. The Altar, now set with items representing each of the five elements, pulsed and ebbed with the powers held within the items.

Once the last available item had been placed on the Altar, they turned and proceeded to the edge of the clearing. They each pulled their dagger across their palms, their blood dropping into the dirt as they lifted their arms to the side to form a circle. Raising their faces to the full moon above, they began to chant a spell of protection, their remaining magic rising around them. Their bodies swayed with the magic and as their soft voices carried through the woods, a circle of protection formed. A circle that would only reveal the clearing and open again in twenty years for each of the families' second born descendants to enter. These twelve would be able to release the magic inside using only a drop of their own blood. They would return the powers to their kin before guarding the items placed in the clearing.

The spell complete, they dropped their arms and looked at each other, exhaustion clear in their eyes. In silent acknowledgement they turned away from each other. They knew that once they left the clearing, they would no longer be siblings in the craft but would be near powerless strangers. Soon they would leave Salem forever to start anew in safer territories far from all they knew and far from one another. Their powers would only return to them once the clearing was opened by the chosen descendants in twenty years.

CHAPTER 1

I WOKE WITH A stretch and a yawn, smiling at the sky brightening through the sheer white curtains of my bedroom window. Pulling them open, the morning sun filled and began to warm my room. I dressed for the day in a pair of light blue jeans and a thin navy-blue long sleeve shirt. Pulling the elastic from the end of my braid and running my fingers through the waves before I picked up my brush and pulled the garnet-colored strands into a low ponytail. Giving my hair a tightening tug, I headed from my bedroom and padded down the stairs past the multitude of family pictures. I brushed my fingers over the old worn wood of the Triple Moon sculpture that hung on the wall at the bottom of the stairs, the familiarity and comfort of the act made me smile softly. Stepping from the stairs and into the open kitchen and dining room I smiled wider at the flow of my siblings moving about the large space, carrying plates filled with food.

My younger brother Evan leaned against the wall in rumpled jeans and a black Hensley thermal. He was watching the chaos as he shoveled eggs from his heaping plate into his mouth. His dark brown hair was in messy spikes, red showing here and there in the sunlight streaming in through the large sliding doors that led out back. The youngest of us, a set of twin boys were laughing. Their breakfast lay forgotten on the table, as they darted around my oldest brother Aiden. He grabbed them both and gave them a shove towards the door. They grabbed the toast from their plates on the way out. I laughed and shook my head when he met my gaze and rolled his eyes.

Though a year and a half apart in age Aiden and I were often thought to be twins. We both had our father's red hair and green eyes. In addition to the physical similarities, we had a tendency to be able to read each other's mind. It was something we had been doing ever since we were little. It had helped us keep each other out of trouble just as often as it had gotten us into trouble. My mother often joked that had we actually been her first set of twins we would have been her only children.

"Good morning McKenna dear," My mother pressed a kiss to my forehead as she passed me a plate of scrambled eggs with cheese and bacon along with a large chilled glass of orange juice. She had on an ankle length dark green skirt that swirled around her as she moved about the kitchen making breakfast as she did every morning. She wore a white blouse, which was hidden under her favorite midnight blue apron. Her dark brown hair was swept up in a high ponytail and I could see the glimmer of the sapphires in her ears. My father had gotten the earrings for her as a Yule gift several years ago, saying they had reminded him of her eyes when she laughed.

"Morning Momma," I smiled and returned a kiss to her cheek. "Where's daddy?"

"Already out opening up the gate to let the others in," She smiled at me.

I turned and saw Selena was in one of her typical dresses, this one knee length and long sleeved to help with the slight January chill. She had her waist length brown hair braided tightly and was twirling the end around her finger as she leaned against the counter reading while she idly picked at her breakfast. Stepping around her I set the plate and glass on the dining room table. I slipped my feet into my old brown boots and pulled on a jean jacket. I picked my breakfast back up before heading out to the whitewashed porch. The old boards creaked under my feet as I walked towards my favorite spot, the old porch swing. A breeze floated across the porch, swirling the light fragrance of the pansies my mother kept in the window boxes around me. I was only halfway to the swing when a blur of red, green, and white darted from the hedges around the porch and flitted around my head. I laughed and balanced my plate on my glass before holding out a finger for my ruby-throated hummingbird familiar, "Good morning to you too Zipper," I greeted as he landed momentarily.

Zipper chirped and lifted from my finger again to zoom around me. He fluttered his delicate wings faster until my ears filled with their hum. The bouncing garnet curls of my ponytail lifted a little each time he circled behind me making me laugh. When he flitted from my finger again, I picked my plate back up and continued towards the swing. I curled up on the bench seat with my breakfast balanced on my lap, my glass of juice on the porch rail just within reach. Zipper quickly nestled himself in my hair above my ponytail like a living comb. As I ate I watched the ranch yard become a slow buzz of activity as the others in the coven began to arrive to start their day.

Most would be working in the Astral Planes, entering them through the portals in the gazebo and using each plane to check the weaves of our universe. They would promote the health of this year's harvest, help soul mates find each other, assist the supernaturals of the world to grow and harness their powers. They would heal the injured and depressed, inspire the worlds artists and help to find the truths and serve justice. The rest would stay to take care of the youngest children who weren't old enough to travel the Planes and provide teaching to them and the middle kids. I watched as my siblings streamed one after the other from the house running off to tend to their assignments in the planes and here on the mortal plane. Aiden was the last to leave the house.

"Let's move short stuff, we have work to do." He said grinning at me.

"Almost done and then I'll be on my way," I rolled my eyes at him and finished the last bite of toast on my plate. Dusting my fingers over my jeans I stood and walked back into house, empty plate and glass in hand.

"McKenna you know the rules. No familiars in the house!" my mother admonished as I handed her my now empty plate and she saw Zipper nestled above my ponytail, "this place is enough of a zoo without bringing actual animals inside."

"Sorry momma, but he's asleep. I didn't want to wake him, and besides I'm heading out now and none of the others are in here to see him," I smiled as I headed towards the door, "See you at lunch time." I blew her a kiss as I slipped outside. I stopped on the bottom step of the three porch stairs and tipped my face to the sun, enjoying the heat on my pale skin. Taking a deep breath, the smell of grass and fresh earth filling my senses. This was the smell of home.

Opening my eyes, I stepped into the yard and waved at the others as they milled about in the early morning light. I made my way to the octagonal gazebo in the center of the yard where the Portals to the Planes had been established generations before. I could see that the white paint was starting to peel and knew Aiden and I would be tasked with repainting it this spring. As I approached, two of the coven's older children darted from the bright yellow of the third plane into the purple of the seventh plane laughing as they chased each other. I smiled remembering when me and Aiden would chase each other through the Planes, darting through the portals, clueless to the mayhem we caused to those working within them.

I shook my head remembering when we had snuck into the second plane, our curiosity piqued by the single off-limits plane. I had been thirteen and that one trip into the second plane had led to a very awkward discussion between me and my mother about life. She had explained that the second plane was where love happened, where soul mates were led to each other. That when two true soul mates came together, the echoes of their passion could be heard throughout that plane. I hadn't set foot in that plane for three long years after that, and for the first year my cheeks turned red every time I saw anyone entering or leaving the second plane.

Fifteen witches were assigned to every plane, my siblings and I were included in those who worked the planes, though only Aiden and I were able to work the second plane as the others were not old enough yet. I checked the list on the railing of the stairs where my parents posted who would be working where every night and saw that I had been assigned to the fourth Astral Plane today. The fourth plane was where we worked with animals that had been injured in the normal realm. Smiling

I picked up a jug of healing water by the edge of the gazebo and walked up the seven steps. I made my way to the rail of the gazebo across from the stairs as I attached the healing water on to my belt loops. As I stepped up to the railing, I lifted my hand and a swirling green portal opened between me and the railing. I stepped in and blinked, my eyes took a moment to adjust to the slight green haze that tinted this plane.

A few moments later I walked to a paddock and was greeted by a chorus of nickers. Slipping between the rails I made my way through the herd of horses running my hand gently over their backs. Most of the animals who were here would only have minor scrapes and abrasions that wouldn't need tending. Several would have more extensive injuries that would need healing. A few wouldn't be so lucky though. They would be so close to death from injury or illness that the best we would be able to do was comfort them until they passed on. Toward the middle of the paddock I found a paint mare laying on her side and knelt next to her. She had several long gashes running along her stomach and neck, her coat matted with blood. It looked like she had been attacked by a cougar, luckily though it looked like her owners had decided to tend to her wounds and not just put her down.

"Hey sweet baby," I cooed and uncapped the water, "let's see if we can get you back up on your feet, uh?" I dipped my fingers into the cool water and pulled them back out, moving so that the water dripped into the wounds.

The mare snorted in discomfort and shook her head. "I know sweet girl, it doesn't feel good, but it will soon." Once I made sure to spread the healing water into each of the cuts, I traced my wet fingers along the outside of them washing away the blood as best I could. After that was done, I held my hands over them and closed my eyes picturing her whole and unharmed. I felt my palms warm and a light breeze stirred around me. Again, the mare snorted, and I opened my eyes to find that the wounds had begun to close, "There you go hon, you'll be back up and running in no time." I smiled at the mare as she lurched to her feet and slowly ambled away. She would need several more treatments here in the Astral Planes even as she was tended to in the mortal realm, but she would survive. I stood and continued to move through the horses, finding which I could heal quickly and helping them first. Some with just deep scrapes and cuts I would run damp fingers over and the wounds would close instantly. I stopped at a few of the more severe cases between the others and did what I could to ease their pain. My heart ached when I came across a few who were injured due to mistreatment and I sent a prayer to the goddess to help them even as I lingered with them, showing them as much kindness as I could. Zipper stayed nestled in my hair the whole morning, giving me strength whenever I started to feel the drain from the magic.

CHAPTER 2

I STOOD FROM KNEELING next to a small white foal who had been born too early. It had been one that couldn't be saved and I felt tears tracking down my cheeks. Quickly wiping my eyes with the backs of my hands I continued on as there was still about half of the herd to work through. I couldn't stop to mourn the loss of such a young life. Continuing to work my way through the herd, I was thankful that there did not seem to be any other foals amongst the horses. Needing a short break, I made my way over to the fence around the paddock. Crossing my arms on the top rail, I leaned against it and lifted my face to the green tinted sky, closing my eyes to soak in the warmth of the sun. It wasn't as warm as the sun in the mortal realm, but it still felt amazing. A breeze washed over me, swirling the scent of animals and fresh air around me.

Turning back to face the herd of horses I felt a tightening close to my heart, and then a sharp tug in my chest. I was abruptly being pulled back. I reached out and grabbed onto the rail, trying to hold on. As the pulling intensified, my fingers slipped off the rail and I was pulled back through the portal into the mortal realm. I, along with others from other areas within the plane, stumbled back into the gazebo struggling to keep our feet. Zipper whistled indignantly as he fell from the nest he had made in my hair, his wings fluttering madly to keep him from hitting the ground. I watched as he flew up and nested in the rafters.

"I'm sorry Zipper buddy," I cooed at the annoyed bird and held a finger out for him to land on before slipping him back on my shoulder. I helped a few people around me to their feet when they stumbled to their knees. The gazebo had become so crowded we could barely move and still more people came stumbling from the surrounding portals.

The gazebo was quickly overflowing with witches and I looked over and caught Aiden's eyes. He nodded towards where the portal he had just come from was and I nodded in agreement. We needed to try to re-open the portals. I slid between people to stand in front of the gazebo railing where the portal would normally open. I waved my hand, but nothing happened. I looked to either side of me to see my siblings mirroring me and getting the same results.

When we turned around to face the crowd, the younger siblings moved to stand behind the older ones, Aiden, Kristen and me. Question after panicked question were hurled at us, "What's going on?"

"Why won't the Portals open?"

"Why were we kicked out of the Astral Planes?"

I looked at Aiden; we didn't have answers to calm their fears. I watched my brother take a deep breath, "Everyone calm down," he said his deep voice washing over everyone. He stepped forward from between Kristen and me, taking charge of the panicked crowd. Aiden raised his hands in a soothing gesture, "we are not sure what is happening to the portals. We only know what you do, that we were pulled from the Astral Plane and now they won't open again. We need everyone to stay calm and move away from the gazebo onto the grounds to help avoid possible injury. We will go speak with the High Priest and Priestess to see if they have any insight for us. Once there is something to tell you, you will be informed." At his soothing words people began removing themselves from the raised platform of the gazebo.

Once the others had all exited the gazebo my siblings and I followed, Aiden exited last and secured a chain across the entrance. My chest tightened at the click. The crowd from the gazebo had moved to the front of the sanctuary, where others began to join them to find out what had happened. They huddled in small groups on the lawn. As we passed, I could hear panicked whispers coming from the groups as they formed. Aiden led the way and I ushered the others between us so I could bring up the rear of our small group, only Thea who had been working with the children today was missing.

The Sanctuary sat on the opposite side of the gravel parking lot from our house and was a small stucco structure. It had once been the original homestead. As my family's resources grew, they built the house we now lived in. The homestead had first been converted into a schoolhouse for the children's lessons to take place when they became of school age before becoming the sanctuary. It was still sometimes used for that purpose when the weather was bad, but mostly lessons now took place outdoors. It had only been within the last few generations that it had been converted into a place where the coven could gather for Esbats, Holidays and the rare large, complex ritual.

We bypassed the crowd in the front of the building, Aiden led us around the corner to the side entrance. This door was supposed to be reserved for only the Priests and Priestesses to use when entering the building. It was painted a tan the same color as the stucco siding of the building so it blended in, making it hard to see from a distance. Looking to make sure that no one was watching, Aiden opened the door and ushered us all in, closing the door tight behind us. The inside of the building was lit only by the sun that filtered in through the windows. The old wood floor creaked and groaned as we made our way inside and the faint smell of smoke from extinguished candles and incense filled the air as always. I glanced at the front door and felt my worry rise. The doors had been locked. Something my parents never did. The main area was completely empty. In fact, glancing around I noticed the candles on the Altar had not even been lit. This was not a good sign. I turned to look at Aiden.

"Stay here," He said quietly before walking over to the pull down stairs that led to our parents' private chambers above. We all stood in the small dimly lit room in silence, lost in our own thoughts. The side door opened again and Thea stepped in, joining the rest of us. I felt a hand slip into mine and looked over at Kristen. I gave her hand a light squeeze and smiled at her as reassuringly as I could. I saw my own worry reflected in her sky-blue eyes as we waited to learn what was happening I moved the group to sit on one of the benches, before turning and making my way to the altar.

I knelt and reached out to rest my hand on the Goddess statue that was in the center, to the right of the God statue and between the two large black pillar candles. I closed my eyes and let myself feel a breeze of warmth wrap around me as I sent a prayer to the Goddess to help us. Once finished I stood and made my way back to my siblings, the warm breeze clinging to me. I sat on a front bench and my siblings quickly moved to surround me. The younger twins tucked themselves into my side. Kristen sat on the other side of Nathaniel reaching out to link our fingers again, seeking comfort.

"Kenna, what's going on? Why did the Portals close?" Selena asked as she sat on the floor facing me, her knees pulled to her chest, eyes filled with uncharacteristic worry. Thea sat next to Selena, the twins leaning against each other. Thea's head on her twin's shoulder, their arms linking together in solidarity.

"I don't know," I looked around and met each of my younger sibling eyes, "I have never heard of us not being able to enter the Planes or of the portals not opening. Hopefully, Mom and Dad will have answers for us, or ideas at least."

"I'm scared," Zack whispered looking up at me.

"I am too, but we will get through this. Our family always does." I pressed a kiss to his forehead.

"Will you sing for us?" Thea asked.

"Of course," I forced a smile. Closing my eyes I hummed a few bars of the lullaby mom had always sung to us before starting, "Hush little witch, nothing to fear. Pray to the Goddess, she will hear. Mother's arms wrap us tight. The moon high above gives us light. Close your eyes now time to rest, so tomorrow you can do your very best."

I had just finished singing it for the fourth time when we heard Aiden descending the stairs, followed by first our mother then our father. I went to stand but my mother motioned me to stay seated. The three on the floor turned so they could face our parents as Aiden joined us, sitting on the other side of Zackery. Our parents looked at each other then back at us, their hands linked in unity.

CHAPTER 3

"**D**ADDY, WHAT'S GOING ON? Why won't the portals open and why did the Astral Planes kick us out?" I asked softly.

"We don't know yet," he answered, "We just got off a call with all the other Coven Leaders. It isn't just Astral Projection that has stopped working. All of the powers have stopped. Healing, premonitions, teleportation, telekinesis, telepathy, invisibility, illusions, energy fields and time manipulation, all of them. Our communication with the ancestors seems to have also stopped working, so we cannot reach out to them for help either." I looked over to my sibling's eyes wide in shock. How could we have lost all our powers? How would we survive without them?

"What are we going to do?" Kristen asked.

"We" dad motioned to himself and mom, "are going to look through the ancestor's old grimoires to find the spell they would have used to reach the planes before they set up the portals."

"Until we find it, we want you guys to go out and work to calm the coven members. We will send our familiars to get you once we have found something," mom said.

Aiden nodded, "We will do what we can mom but maybe just Kenna, Kristen and I should go out there and leave the younger ones in here."

"I agree, the rest can stay in here. It's safer," I nodded, "I know that we are talking about friends and family but they are starting to panic outside. I say we err on the side of caution."

"We can handle ourselves" Nathaniel argued.

"Of course, you can," my mother soothed, "but if we send all of you out there it could cause more panic. The coven has already accepted your older siblings as coven adults. You will have your time soon enough" She smiled at the youngest two.

"I can run to the house and get a few games for us to play." Evan offered quietly.

"We are hoping it won't take that long," my father said, "but it is kind of you to offer."

I ruffled Evan's hair as I followed Aiden towards the side door, with Kristen behind me.

"Aiden, what are we supposed to tell everyone?" Kristen asked.

"Whatever we can to keep them calm." He pushed open the door and held it as Kristen and I slipped out.

"Ok, well let's split this up. I'll take the right, Aiden you take the center, Kristen you take the left." I said peeking around the corner of the building, "Let's just let the coven know we understand their concerns, we have concerns too. That we don't know what has happened, but that mom and dad are working to learn what they can. We assure them that as soon as mom or dad learn anything, we will all be told. We ask them if we can get anything to help them." I said looking back at the others.

"Since when are you into hostage negotiations little sister?" Aiden asked looking at me as if he had never seen me before.

"This is what happens when you know how to read big brother," I smirked. We all took each other's hands and gave a comforting squeeze before dropping them and heading out to the crowd.

"I agree with your suggestion, but I think first we address them as a group. It should settle some things down." Aiden said softly.

"What about getting them to help us set up some of the summer tents?" Kristen suggested, "we don't know how long they will be here, it will give them something to do and also give shade."

"That's a really good suggestion," Aiden nodded.

"Ok, Kristen and I will answer questions. Aiden you organize and help set up the tents." I suggested, reorganizing my earlier plan. The others nodded their agreement.

As soon as we stepped around the building we were bombarded with questions, "Please everyone," Aiden spoke up, his deeper baritone voice carrying over the crowd better than Kristen's or mine would have, "We will come around and try to answer your individual questions the best we can. Currently, we do not know much, but the High Priest and Priestess are working to learn more. Once they know more, they will tell all of us." He waited a few moments for everyone to process his words, "We would like to set up a couple of the summer tents and are asking for help from any one here who can. Anyone who is able to help with that if you could please follow me to the barn." With that Aiden ended his speech. Several people stepped forward to follow him to the barn while Kristen and I dispersed ourselves into the remaining crowd.

Despite Aiden telling the group that we did not know much, I was still asked several dozen times about what had happened to our powers. I explained that we were not sure how or why, but that it was being looked into. I got a few of the older coven members chairs from inside the Sanctuary, placing them under the tents that Aiden and the others had erected. After about 30 minutes I ducked my head back into the Sanctuary and tasked Thea and Selena with bringing out and setting up chairs and also a table with glasses of water and lemonade on it.

A few of the younger kids had lost their families in the crowd and I helped to calm the tears before we located their equally frantic parents. I made a mental note to talk to mom and dad about having the middle kids start a mini daycare tent if things continued for too much longer. I ran into a few of my aunts and uncles, stopping and pulling them aside to give them a little deeper information in hushed tones, as I knew my parents would approve and that they would not spread the news to the others. If the coven figured out that we had lost all of our powers before we had a plan to get them back there would be chaos.

By the time I felt Snowball, my mother's familiar, a white miniature poodle, pawing at my legs the once nervous and roiling crowd had calmed. Though I could feel their energy leaning back toward the turbulent side as I followed the white canine back inside. I gave everyone reassuring smiles and squeezed their shoulders in solidarity as I passed through to keep the crowd from panicking again. Our Parents stood side by side at the front of the Sanctuary when we walked inside.

"Mom, dad, what did you guys learn?" Aiden asked when the door closed behind us.

"Not as much as we hoped," Mom said softly.

"We will tell you and the coven all at once what we have learned," Dad said resting a hand on his shoulder, "we don't want to keep the coven waiting any longer than we already have. You have calmed them some, but if we leave them without information much longer, they will begin to panic again." With that they led us all out the front doors to face the coven once again.

"Please everyone, be calm" my father's voice rang out and the crowd went silent. He looked to my mother and she took his hand in solidarity.

"We have received news from the other covens," mom said. Her voice wasn't as loud as my fathers but still carried across the quiet crowd, "The ability to walk the Astral Planes is not the only power lost, as I am sure some of you have noticed. All of our powers seem to have stopped working," She paused as the noise rose in panic again. "However," again my mother's voice carried with the same tone she had taken with us children. The coven quieted, much like my siblings and I had done many times before, "However, several of the covens have found the ancient methods to still be viable, at least for a few of their members."

"What does that mean?" A voice called out from the crowd.

"It means," My father stepped forward and took over, "that as the Shadow Watch Coven, we have to try to reach the Astral Planes." He stopped letting the noise rise and fall again before continuing to speak, "It is our duty as descendants of the first Plane Walker. We are going to try to reach the Planes ourselves. If we do not succeed, we will need every family in the coven to try. After searching through old Grimoires and Books of Shadows, we were able to find a ritual that we will use to try to reach the Planes. If we are unsuccessful, we will need help from the Coven. We ask that the eldest of each family step forward to try and reach the Astral Planes. We will also need a second member of each family to act as an anchor," He paused to let the news settle across the families, "We will only do about half of us today and the rest tomorrow. We need those volunteering from each family to come to the sanctuary after lunch. Those who are not participating in the ritual today, we would be grateful if you would lend yourself to form a circle of protection around the sanctuary."

Mom took over again with her reassuring smile, "Now, go and spend time with your families, we will send word to those who we would like to come today." With that they both turned and motioned us back into the sanctuary. Once the family was all inside, they closed the doors and turned to face my seven siblings and me.

CHAPTER 4

"IF YOUR FATHER AND I don't succeed, as the oldest, Aiden, we will need you to try with the others." My mother said stepping forward to rest a hand on my brother's arm, the other reaching up to cup his cheek.

"We can't guarantee anyone's safety during this." My father said. He moved up to stand behind my mother, "It has been too long since any of us have tried to reach the Astral Plane by any means other than through a stable portal. One of your siblings will act as an anchor to hold you to this plane, but unfortunately that is the most help anyone can give you."

"I understand," Aiden squeezed my mother's hand lightly before leaning down to kiss her cheek. He turned to look at the seven of us standing behind them. I felt my chest tighten at the thought of losing my brother, my friend, my confidant. Without thought I stepped forward from the crowd, standing between my younger siblings and the oldest three of the family.

"I'll do it," I said, my voice surprisingly clear and steady, "I'll anchor you Aiden. Since I'm the second born, one of the more experienced of us, it only makes sense for me to be the one. Not to mention, Aiden and I have worked the most spells together," I watched my mother's eyes fill with tears, but she nodded. I stepped up next to him like I had so many times before, to stand by his side like I always had and always would. Aiden looked over at me and nodded his head once, reaching out to take my hand. As he did a soft rush of power swept around us before dying out again. We would be in this together, like we had through so many things in our lives.

My father coughed softly as if trying to clear his throat, "We need to prepare the space, there will soon be a lot of people in here trying to call a lot of magic," His voice rasped as if he was holding back emotions. "We need you all to clear this room out and gather the list of supplies we wrote out for you. Your mother and I need to go back upstairs to attempt to reach the Planes. If we are lucky, we will be able to find a way there and all of this work will be for nothing."

"If we are lucky, the two of you will not need to risk yourselves." My mother said hugging both Aiden and I tight to her before she handed me the list of supplies and followed my father back to their office.

The first thing we did was clear the large area of the Sanctuary. The chairs were moved along the outer edges and stacked. The few benches from the front of the room were put in front of the stacked chairs. The younger kids were sent to the cellar to fetch the listed supplies that we needed. While we worked, my parents began to call magic to the small office above the Sanctuary. We could hear them chanting faintly above us as we worked and felt their magic swirling around us like a comforting blanket.

A few hours later I stopped Aiden with a hand on his shoulder in a corner farthest away from where our siblings congregated around the boxes of supplies, "Are you sure about this?"

"Honestly, I'm terrified." He answered quietly, running a hand through his hair as he watched our siblings, "but I know that it's something we need done."

"I'll be with you the entire time."

"I know," he smiled down at me, "I could play it big and tough, but honestly I feel better knowing that you're going to be the one doing this with me. We have worked together so often, and besides the twins, we read each other the best."

I nodded in understanding, "I'll hopefully be able to tell if anything starts to go wrong and pull you out of the spell."

"Exactly. It's not that I don't trust our sibling's magic to hold me here. I just am glad to have you by my side during this."

"Like I would let you get into trouble without me," I grinned and shoved his shoulder trying to lighten the mood.

My father's exhaustion ladened voice called down from the office, "Aiden, McKenna, can you please join us up here?" We both walked over to the fold down stairs and made our way up to the office. Mom and Dad's office had once been the attic of the old homestead, but it had now been completely finished. There were skylights in the slanted roof to provide light to the room through most hours of the day and low oak bookshelves around the room provided plenty of storage for the generations worth of coven archives. In front of two of the four windows, worked into the shelves were two desks. This was where our parents worked throughout the day. Off to the side of the hatch under one of the skylights was a low altar made of wood that had been worn smooth from use over the centuries. Mom knelt in front of the altar, clearing off several burned down candles. Both our parents looked completely exhausted. Dad ushered us over to the altar and we sat on either side of mom as he sat across from her.

"This is Sara Osborn's Grimoire" Mom said, her voice soft, motioning to an old small worn leather book, "Sara brought our family, our coven here from Salem after escaping the witch trials. She also started the tradition in our coven of every witch writing both their own Grimoire and their own Book of Shadows. Before her, one Grimoire and one Book of

Shadows was passed from parents to the oldest child. Sara allowed her children to copy from her Grimoire any spell they wished before adding their own. Yet none of her children chose to copy down the spell needed to reach the Planes. We assume this was because the portals were already in place. This means that in this book is the only copy we have of the spell they used to use to reach the Planes before they established the Portals. What we learned from Sara's Book of Shadows is that if one dies in any of the Astral Planes, they cannot be revived on this plane. Their body will remain alive but there will be no way to wake them. So, if you gain access to the Astral Plane you must be careful and return immediately to your body. Once we know someone is able to reach the Planes we can go from there."

"Mom if there is only one copy how are there supposed to be over forty witches saying this spell all at once?" I asked, "Are we going to make copies of it?"

"No, we've decided that the two of you will start first, and from there your father and I will go from pair to pair and help them with both the words and the ritual. Once everyone is started, we will pray to the Goddess that one of you are able to get through." The last was said quietly, as if only for herself.

After a moment of silence, we all descended to the main sanctuary where the younger kids had around 40 sets of supplies spread out across the floor. There was also one on the slightly raised platform in the front. This is where Aiden and I would be. Kristen and the other children had also retrieved baskets of food which they had set out and we all sat in a circle and began to eat silently.

I looked across the small table that we were using for an altar and into my brother's emerald eyes, my eyes. We had been in this same position many times before. This time was different though in more ways than one. Most times when we sat like this we were alone with no one watching and working a spell we had written ourselves. Never had we done a ritual that had such dire consequences if it didn't work.

I took a breath to try to slow my racing heart. I felt hundreds of eyes on us, watching and waiting, reminding me again just what was on the line. It took everything I had to keep my back straight and not shrink under the weight of so many people watching. These were neighbors and friends, I kept reminding myself, not strangers or enemies.

Faintly I could hear chanting outside the walls of the sanctuary. The rest of the coven was raising a circle of protection around the Sanctuary, their voices blending as power swelled around us. They would be protecting us all as we tried to gain entrance to the Planes.

My mother's voice washed over and around me, bringing me back from my thoughts as she explained to the others what they would be doing. Aiden and I had memorized both the ritual and the incantation over the last hour as we poured over Sara's grimoire side by side. Suddenly my father was there, and I looked up at him startling slightly as he took my trembling hand in his. He gave it a soft squeeze of reassurance. I looked down as he turned my palm up and slid the point of his dagger across it. He reached across me, and I watched as he took my other hand and repeated the process. I took a sharp breath through my nose at the bite of the blade both times and hissed as the pain flared like a line of fire. I watched as he did the same across Aiden's right palm. I reached my left hand across the table, and we clasped hands, our blood mingling on our skin. We each took a long and thin lit stick from my mother and lit the candles that took up most of the small Altar. I held it with fingertips to keep it away from the weeping wound on my hand as I lit the candles. We had one chime candle in each of the colors of the Astral Plane in a circle. Inside that circle were larger black, white, dark blue and royal purple pillar candles in the center of the table where the directional corner candles would normally go.

As the last candle was lit, we looked up and gave each other the slightest nod. Taking a deep breath each, we closed our eyes. I tightened my grip on Aiden's hand and plunged my free hand into the bowl of salt and earth grimacing at the sharp pains as the small granules slid along the cut in my hand. I heard Aiden begin the incantation, his words coming out a breathy whisper, that barely reached my ears.

I felt our parents move away and a second later I sensed the pull of Aiden's power. I had to clench my teeth to stop from gasping at the sensation. Tears sprung to my eyes, and I hunched my shoulders against the sensation. It was as though someone was pulling a string from the wound in my palm with excruciating slowness. Concentrating more I was aware of that same pull moving into my other hand from the bowl of salt and earth. Taking slow deep breaths, I straightened my shoulders and could feel the string of grounding power run through my body from the bowl of salt and earth and into Aiden where our hands were clasped, tying us together. Taking another deep breath, I forced myself to relax into the power and ignore the pulling and tugging through my body. I focused instead on wrapping my own will and magic around the thread, strengthening it and the hold I had on my brother's subconscious. I pictured the thin line of power wrapping itself around our clasped hands, a glowing gold thread, before it moved back into Aiden's hand. I felt a flutter of wings and then the lightweight of Zipper landing on the wrist of the hand in Aiden's and the pain lessened. The line I had on Aiden strengthened. There was a press of fur against that same side, and the bond I had with my brother strengthen even more. His familiar, a Fennec Fox he had named Jax, had joined us.

I tightened my physical hold on his hand and that's when I started to hear soft whispers in my head. I then felt a hand brushing along my hair, as if someone had walked behind me and dragged their fingertips through the strands. I fought to keep my eyes closed and focused, to not look around for things that I knew couldn't possibly be there. Anyone who was actually in the room would never try to distract someone in the middle of a ritual that was so unknown and even if they had tried, my parents would have stopped them. I had to ignore the low voices even as they beckoned to me, their mystery calling for me to search for them.

CHAPTER 5

WHAT SEEMED LIKE ONLY minutes later I felt soft hands on mine, pulling Aiden and me apart. My mother's gentle voice was telling him it was ok to come back to us. I waited to open my eyes until I felt them pull our hands from each other, the voices faded away completely as they did. When I did open them, I saw that the seven small chime candles had burned completely. We had been trying for over two hours to reach the Planes. I slumped slightly, suddenly exhausted. Wincing as Kristen began to clean and bandage our hands, I ran a finger over Zipper's head, the little bird looking up at me. I lifted him to my shoulder, and he quickly nestled into my hair. He too had felt the drain of energy from the spell. I waited until Kristen was gone, and Evan had placed the small plate of cheese and fruit in front of us, before I looked over at Aiden, hopeful he could give me good news. I felt my heart drop when instead he grimaced and shook his head slightly.

I pulled my knees to my chest and nibbled on the light food, Zipper resting on the back of my neck, under my hair. I watched as my parents brought back and separated the others as their candles burned out as well. My siblings followed behind them to tend to the wounds and deliver food to help refuel them. The feeling of hopelessness and dread settled heavier over me as one after another I saw the slight shake of heads from the oldest to the anchor.

"Aiden," I kept my voice quiet, just above a whisper so I knew he could hear me, and tried to sound calm, "I don't think anyone was able to reach the Planes" I looked over at him. Our eyes met and I saw my emotions mirrored in his. About an hour after they had pulled me and Aiden back to ourselves our parents both walked back to the raised platform where we sat. They stood in front of us, between us and the others, and waited for the rest of the coven to file in when Nathaniel and Zachery opened the door and called to Thea and Selena who led the group in.

"Well, were we successful?" A voice called hesitantly from the crowd funneling in.

"Unfortunately, no one was able to reach the Astral Planes," My father said his voice even and calm. "This means tomorrow we will need the rest of you to join us here to try to reach the Planes. "

My mother spoke up then taking over for him. Her voice was softer but just as calm as his had been, "We thank those of you who stepped up today and those who will come forward tomorrow, we could not do this without all of the covens help. Thank you for helping us to try to fulfill the promise our ancestors made to the Goddess. We suggest that all of you go back to your homes, spend this time with each other, family and friends. This is not a time of ease and we know this. All we ask is that no one panics and remember that we as a coven can make it through anything when we have each other. Let us know if any of you need anything at all and we will do what we can to help. Please help those weakened to make it home and Blessed Be."

A resounding "Blessed Be" rang through the room and I watched as everyone emptied out. Once they had all left the doors were again closed and locked. Aiden and I were helped to our feet. We all exited slowly through the side door and made our way to the house. Dad slipped his arm around Aiden and Kristen stepped up to help support me on our way to the house, both of us still weak from the spell. A few times my feet didn't lift as high as I had meant them to and I stumbled forward when my toe caught on something. Kristen's arm around my waist was the only thing that kept me upright. After the second stumble, Zipper chose to fly above my head instead of staying curled up in my hair.

I shook my head trying to clear the cobwebs that seem to fill it as we walked across the yard. Now I understood why my parents had looked so tired when we had gone up to their office earlier that day. I thought back over the spell work that I had done over the years, and I could not remember ever feeling so dead on my feet. Especially ones where two witches worked in unison. Normally you left a spell like that feeling more energized than when you started since you were sharing energy between the two witches. I couldn't imagine needing to do this every time we wanted to enter the Planes. Feeling this drained at the end of every day, and not even having a sense of security while in the Planes? We definitely had to find a way to get the portals back online.

With no Planes to attend to that evening Aiden and I were helped to the couches in the living room. A blanket was placed around each of our shoulders as I started to shiver. I slunk down and rested my head on the arm of the couch, every inch of my body feeling heavy. Zipper fluttered in and nestled into my hair, I could feel as he dropped into a deep sleep almost immediately. I felt completely drained and my eyes slowly drifted closed as I listened to the others move silently through the kitchen preparing supper. The everyday noises were lulling me into the beckoning silence of sleep.

My mother woke me with a gentle shake of my shoulders, calling my name. When I blinked my eyes to look up at her she slipped her arm around me and helped me to sit up.

"Supper is ready Kenna dear," her voice was soft, eyes gentle. I yawned and nodded my understanding. As she moved over to wake Aiden, I slowly stood stretching my body, muscles feeling tight. I made my way to the dinner table where the rest of the family waited for us. I gave the young ones a soft reassuring smile when they looked up at me with their eyes full of concern. I sat in my usual spot between Kristen and Nathaniel giving each of their hands reassuring squeezes. Aiden and mom joined us shortly and we began passing bowls and filling plates. Mom made spaghetti with choice of chicken or meatballs and her homemade garlic cheesy bread. Once our plates were filled, we began to eat.

The dinner was unusually quiet for us. The younger twins didn't even try to start their normal food fight from across the table. Unsurprisingly, when the plates had been emptied and the table cleared, most of us decided to call it an early night. We all helped to clean up from dinner as quickly as possible before making our way upstairs to our rooms. I walked into my room, where the fading sun from the window above my bed turned the white walls a red orange hue. I changed into my favorite pajama shorts and tank top. Kneeling on the bed I pulled down the rarely used blinds to block out the rest of the light from outside before sliding under the thin pink quilt.

I laid in bed and listened as each of my siblings closed their doors. Next door I could hear Thea and Selena settling into their nightly routine, Thea climbing into the top bunk. I could hear the younger twins murmuring from their room across the hall, only stopping after mom told them it was time for lights out. Outside my door Dad murmured low under his breath, mom responding as they moved down the hall to their room. I rolled from side to side on my bed before finally finding a comfortable position and falling asleep.

CHAPTER 6

A S THE SUN ROSE, I woke up and rolled over with a groan, burying my face in my pillow. I had never hated mornings, but with everything seeming so hopeless the thought of getting out of bed held no appeal to me. Not to mention, I could still feel the residual effects from the spell.

There was a knock on my door, and I lifted my head from the pillows with a groan, "Come on sleepy head, time to get up." My mom's voice floated through my door. Sighing in defeat I sat up and slipped from my bed. I pulled on a pair of dark blue jeans and a white long-sleeved top. My muscles ached as I pulled my hair up into a bun at the back of my head and headed down the stairs. Everyone was still sitting around the table picking at their breakfast when I sat down and stared at my own plate that had a pile of pancakes and several sausage links.

"Mom what are we supposed to do today?" Kristen asked her voice quiet.

"Well at noon, the other coven members will be coming to the sanctuary to see if any of them are able to reach the Planes. Until then, the rest of us will find work around the ranch to do." She answered, "There is work to be done even if we cannot reach the Astral Planes. There are gardens and fields that need to be attended to. Not to mention the animals here wouldn't mind the extra attention."

"Dad, could we do some blade practice this morning?" I asked, "I know the things mother has mentioned are important, plus many other things," I thought about the faded paint on a lot of the fences and the now vacant gazebo and suppressed a shudder, "But we haven't been able to drag the targets out recently. Plus it would be good to practice and for some of the younger kids to start learning."

"That's actually a good idea Kenna," My dad smiled at me, "I will set things up in the back after breakfast."

"Suck up." Aiden whispered grinning at me. I rolled my eyes and stuck my tongue out at him.

"OK you guys, if you are going to be throwing pointy things you need to eat up," mom said smiling at us. Grinning back at her I felt my appetite kick in a little and started eating, excited again about what the day would bring.

An hour later we were all outside behind the empty gazebo. Dad set up a table and several old large wooden targets. On the table were several types of blades ranging from throwing blades to small daggers to fencing rapiers and even two large broad swords. On a second table he had set out a few sharpening kits. When we finished setting up the tables, I sat in the grass with my favorite set of throwing daggers and the dagger that I kept tucked in my boot at all times before me. I gave them a thorough cleaning and sharpening. The movements were a calming repetition that I let myself sink into. Once I could see the sun glinting from their edges I tucked the kits away, ready to get started on the real fun.

I stood several yards from one of the targets and balanced a dagger in my right hand. Taking a deep breath, I focused on the center of the target. Bringing my hand back towards me, I exhaled slowly and threw the blade. After several somersaults through the air, it landed on the thin line between the center ring and the center.

"Good Kenna, try to keep your body a little straighter when you throw." My father said from the other end of the set of tables. He was working to teach proper blade safety to the younger twins, and the younger coven kids who had shown up shortly after we had started. He had spent the first 30 minutes or so showing my younger siblings how to properly sharpen their own blades. We all had the safety talks around our 10th birthday when we were gifted our first athame. When we got our first daggers around our 13th birthday, we again had safety talks. This would be one of the first times Nathaniel and Zackery would be allowed to work on their throwing and the thought was a little worrisome.

I smiled at him and walked to the target. I braced my hand at the top of the chipped wooden circle and pulled the blade free with a hard tug. Zipper flitted around my head as I walked back to the where I had started. I laughed at the small bird, "You silly boy, one of these days you're gonna get a wing clipped." I continued to throw the blade over and over as the sun climbed higher in the sky, until my arms started to tire. Each throw landing within the two center circles.

"Hey, Kenna, wanna duel?" Jake, a classmate from my school years, asked lifting one of the fencing rapiers from the table.

"You really want me to embarrass you in front of all these people Jake?" I smirked.

"Bring it on little girl," he grinned.

I stepped into the circle area dad had outlined with sand. I stopped and rolled my neck before pulling the face mask down.

"You ready?" Jake asked stepping into the circle and smirking at me. I lifted my rapier in one hand in response before beckoning him closer with a curling of my fingers on the other hand. He pulled his mask down and we stepped into each other. Soon the area was filled with the tinging sound of metal on metal as our blades met over and over again. I grinned behind my mask as I spun on the heel of my foot out of the way of his thrusting blade. I continued the circle and brought my sword down to stop at the back of his exposed neck. The crowd that had gathered around us cheered and I tucked the blade under my arm offering my hand for Jake to shake.

"You got me with that one, I forgot how sneaky you could be," he laughed.

"Alright everyone, let's get things cleaned up, lunch will be set up soon in the sanctuary. After we eat, we will need to begin setting up for today's ritual," Dad called with a clap of his hands.

I walked with Jake to the table where we began stripping off the protective gear we had worn, "Are you doing the ritual today for your family?" I asked him quietly as we all started to helped to put away the blades, the table and the targets.

"Yeah, dad wanted to but I pointed out he was technically the youngest of his siblings and thus wouldn't qualify. He wasn't happy but he agreed."

"Good luck to you then," I said putting a hand on his shoulder, "And Jake?"

"Yeah," he looked back at me.

"Be careful, this isn't the spell work we are used to. I can still feel it," I said as he nodded in understanding and we parted ways.

"Hey, you're getting better you know," Aiden said as he walked beside me toward the Sanctuary.

I grinned at him, "soon you won't have the best aim in the family, big brother. Next time you can try challenging me to a duel and lose."

He laughed and tugged my mussed bun, "you wish little sister, you wish."

I knelt next to two of the coven members and dragged my dagger point across their palms, "Ok now join hands and light the candles." I watched as they did as I directed. I nodded encouragingly, "Place your free hand in the bowl and you both need to close your eyes. Now Danny I need you to repeat these words, you can't stop until we tell you or until you reach the First Plane. 'libera ferri, sphaerae, quaerere, ibi me accipere'." I listened as he recited the words and corrected him a few times till I was confident he had the pronunciation down. Then I slowly stood and made my way to the next group. Unlike yesterday where only my mom and dad were helping the others with the ritual Aiden and I were going to each group to help them too. Kristen and Evan were out with the rest of the coven, holding the protective circle around us. Both sets of twins were in the small kitchenette preparing for when the rituals ended. Once the last pair was chanting softly I moved to lean against the Sanctuary doors to watch them all. Aiden soon joined me as our parents walked past the pairs, checking on them, throughout the sanctuary.

"Do we think one of them will get through?" I asked softly looking up at my big brother.

"I really hope so." He replied.

As the hours wore on, we both slid down the doors to sit on the floor. We watched as slowly table after table had smoke rise to the ceiling as their candles extinguished. It took several before Aiden and I had to step in, coaxing the eldest back to us and separating them from their anchor. Once we were sure that each pair was back with us, we then asked if they had reached the Planes. Then we stepped back to let others take over cleaning and feeding them. When the last pair had separated Aiden and I walked over to our parents and reported that none had reached the Planes again today. My heart clenched as Thea and Selena opened the doors and again those from outside flooded in.

My parents waited until everyone was inside before my mother began to speak, "Again we would like to thank all those who tried to reach the Astral Planes. Sadly no one was able to reach the Planes again today," I took Kristen and Aiden's hands in mine, squeezing them.

The announcement was met with a wave of panicked questions. My father waited until the noise died down again to continue for my mother, "This does not mean we will stop trying. We will be reaching out to other covens again. We will see if anyone has any words from their ancestors to help us, or if any have means of reaching out to them for assistance. We will let you know if we learn of anything. Please go in peace and spend time with your families." My father dismissed the coven, and we all made our way back to the house.

CHAPTER 7

MAKING DINNER THAT NIGHT was a family event. Dad made burgers and chicken on the grill. The smoke from the grill carried the smell of the cooking meat to the rest of us as we completed our own tasks. Mom and Kristen made several summer pastas in the kitchen while Thea and I husked corn out on the back porch. Aiden and Selena set up a table for all of us outside and Evan helped Nathaniel and Zackery clean up the Sanctuary. When the food was done, we all sat around the table and enjoyed the cool air.

"Momma, Daddy, what happens if no one can reach the Astral Planes again?" Thea asked once all the plates had been filled. I watched as our parents looked at each other, a conversation in a glance.

"Well," My mother took a deep breath and set her fork down, "I won't tell you everything will be fine. We honestly don't know for sure. We know that back when our ancestors came here, they had been locked away from the Astral Planes for ten years. Once they had settled here, they were locked out for another ten before they were able to set up the portals that we use today. In those twenty years, we can find in history a number of natural disasters. We aren't sure if they were because we couldn't reach the planes or if it was just a coincidence. For the last 300 years our coven has been tending to the Astral Planes every day. So, we do not know what will happen if no one ever goes in them again."

"And we are going to do our best not to find out." My father said putting his hand over my mothers and giving the rest of us a forced smile, as if to reassure us.

"But, if we can't, t-t-things will go bad right?" Thea asked, her voice quivering. Aiden hooked his arm around her shoulders and gave them a small squeeze.

"It will all work out Thea," he said, "As dad said earlier, we are working with other covens and will find a way to get back to the Planes, ok?" she nodded, her eyes wide and shiny.

"If for some reason we cant get into the Planes we will reach out to the Water Nation Elves, many of them posses the ability to walk the Planes," Mom said.

"Mom I thought elves were dangerous and untrustworthy." Evan cut it.

"Some," mom nodded, "the same way that some witches are and some shifters are. But there is good in every type of people. You all have studied the witch trials, you know that even humans can be dangerous."

"Will we become completely mortal like the humans?" Zackary asked.

"No darling. Even though we have lost the high powers we will always have our more innate abilities, those that we are born with. We will always have a closer tie with nature than the humans do." She stopped and looked around the table at all of us, "Children, we are witches no matter what happens. We will find a way to continue to serve the Goddess and nature even if we do not have our higher powers."

"How mom?" Selena asked.

"We will turn back to the old ways of spells and start relearning in depth herbalism. Our ancestors used to only have access to one high power per coven, most of the rest were able to be emulated with nature." She took a deep breath, "It will not be easy my darlings, but we are strong." She took Selena's hand in her left and Thea's in her right. I took Evan's hand in my left and Zackery's in my right, as Aiden did the same with Kristen and Selena. Soon we were all connected around the table in a circle.

"We are still powerful witches," Dad said softly as power began to build around us. It felt like a warm soft current passing through us from hand to hand. A gentle breeze wrapping around us in the opposite direction. I started to smile at Zackery but then I heard the soft beckoning whispers again and the smile faltered. Instead I looked past dad toward the Sanctuary and could have sworn I saw a figure swirling in red. It was for only a moment then the figure seemed to be swept away in the current of magic that swept around my family and me.

My mother's voice jerked me back to myself, "See my loves, we still have powers" she said softly to us. We all dropped hands and the breeze around us subsided. And we soon went back to dinner, the atmosphere around the table less depressed than it had been to start.

After dinner was finished and the table had been cleared, Dad started a fire in the small fire pit to the side of the house. Mom retrieved her now seldomly used guitar from its corner in the living room, and she played as we sang the songs she had taught us when we were younger. My siblings smiled and laughed freely, but I couldn't help the unease I felt and had to fight not to look towards the sanctuary. It was well into the night before we all made our way into the house and up to bed. Dad and Aiden carried the youngest twins who had fallen asleep.

I sat on my bed, back resting against the wall as I listened to my family settle in their beds and drift off to sleep. I looked out my window towards the darkened sanctuary, and all I could think of was the swirling red figure that I has seen during dinner. I stretched out on my bed laying down and closed my eyes, willing myself to sleep. Even as I mentally hummed the songs I had spent all night singing, the beckoning whispers rang louder in my head. When I could no longer fool myself into believing that I could sleep I slid from bed and crossed to the door. Peeking through the crack, I confirmed the other six doors were all closed. I crept out into the hallway. I crept silently through the moonlight hallway and down the darkened stairs. I stopped, pressing my palm to the Triple Moon sculpture sending a prayer up to the Goddess for help and protection. I pulled on my boots and slid my coat on over my pajamas. I slipped out the door and was met by a questioning whistle.

"Quiet Zipper," I whispered. Sticking to the shadows, I made my way to the sanctuary with Zipper following with a silent hum of his wings.

CHAPTER 8

I QUIETLY SLIPPED IN through the unlocked side door and closed it behind me. I rested my back against the door. Zipper settled on my shoulder, a comforting presence. I took a few minutes letting my eyes adjust to the near total darkness in the room. The only light was from the moon beams streaming through the windows. Once I was sure I could walk through the still cluttered room without tripping over anything, I walked over to where the twins had stacked the boxes of unused candles along one wall. I rifled through them. I pulled out the necessary candles and set them next to me in a small pile. Gathering all the supplies I made my way back to the same cushion I had occupied the day before and sat.

I pulled my dagger from my coat pocket and used it to scrape the old candles from the table as they had adhered themselves as they melted. I replaced them with new ones, each over its melted predecessor. Zipper lifted himself from my shoulder as I began to light the candles. I started at the chime candle farthest from me and my way around the seven outer candles before lighting the four taller pillar candles. As each candle's wick caught, the room seemed to grow warmer and brighter. The flames of the candles were the only light in the dark building.

I filled the two bowls I had set on either side of me with the mix of salt and earth. Taking a deep breath, I slid the tip of my dagger across my palms reopening the barely scabbed over skin, and hissed at the pain. I closed my eyes, plunged my hands deep into two bowls of earth and salt, grimacing as I felt the small granules again scrape and fill the open wounds on my hands. Breathing past the pain I began the chant Aiden had said yesterday, "libera ferri, sphaerae, quaerere, ibi me accipere" Over and over I chanted the words as the small hummingbird settled on my lap, adding his strength to mine.

I began to feel like I was being stretched. There was one force pulling me up and an equal force stringing from palm to palm through my body keeping me grounded on this Plane. I heard the faint whispers again even as I felt myself being pulled in opposite directions. I realized then, that by trying to anchor myself, I was actually preventing the spell from working. I pulled my hands from the bowls, the strands of grounding magic releasing as the salt and earth fell from the wounds on my palms. Raising my voice, I repeated the incantation once again. I felt myself being pulled up and then suddenly I was no longer seated in the sanctuary, instead stumbling forward nearly tripping over the small table.

My eyes flew open and I blinked rapidly in an attempt to orientate myself. Everything around me was red. I was in the first Astral Plane. Slowly I spun around, taking in my surroundings. I cautiously made my way to the window of the Sanctuary and peeked out. The first Plane was used to nurture basic needs, clean air, healthy soil, clean water. It didn't look much different from the last time I had been here but there seemed to be a wrongness to the air. I heard what sounded like branches scratching against the side of the Sanctuary and my mom's words began echoing in my head, 'if one dies in any of the Astral Planes, they cannot be revived on the mortal plane. Their body will remain alive but there will be no way to wake them.' A loud bang sounded against the sanctuary doors and I jumped, my heart racing. I rushed back to the still burning candles on the altar and knelt. Closing my eyes, I thought of home and felt a sudden rush downward. My eyes jerked open and once again I was back home in the dark sanctuary. I looked down to see Zipper looking up at me, my heart thudding in my chest. I scooped the small bird into my hand before scrambling to my feet. I quickly extinguished the candles, all but the large white pillar keeping that one to help my vision. Carrying the candle to the side door I reached for the handle. Before I could open it I remembered the scratching and the banging on the front door I had heard in the Plane and hesitated. I took a deep breath and pulled the door open. I ran back to the house, not looking back to see if there was anything behind me. Once safely inside I blew out the candle and set it on the table before rushing upstairs to wake my parents.

As I passed his room Aiden stuck his head out, "Everything ok Kenna?" His voice was thick with sleep.

"Let me get mom and dad and we will all meet downstairs," I said not slowing or looking back.

CHAPTER 9

ONCE MY PARENTS WERE awake and downstairs, I told them what happened in the Sanctuary. They all stood around the kitchen as I paced. When I finished, I stopped and stood in the middle of the kitchen, my parents and Aiden looking at me like I had just told them the impossible.

"I'm going to make us some coffee," Mom said laying a gentle hand on Dad's arm before moving into the kitchen.

"Tell us again what you did." My father said running a hand over his face before running it through his hair as if he were still trying to wake up.

I took a deep breath and fell into one of the chairs before starting again, "When I was anchoring Aiden yesterday, I heard things. They were like voices whispering to me, and I swore I felt something brush against my hair. After dinner tonight when we went to bed I couldn't sleep, all I could think about were the voices and the feeling through my hair." I looked up at them, needing them to believe me and understand, "I knew reaching the Astral Planes was important, so I snuck back out to the sanctuary. I set up the Altar like we had before and placed both my hands into bowls of salt and earth to ground myself and then I said the incantation. I felt like I was being stretched, like something was trying to pull me up while something else was also holding me down." I stood and paced the dining room again as I thought back, "I think by trying to anchor myself I limited my ability to move from this Plane. When I removed my hands from the bowls it felt like I was pulled straight up and suddenly I was in the first plane." I looked up at the three of them and sent a prayer to the Goddess that they would believe me.

"You do realize how irresponsible it was for you to do this alone don't you?" My mother said coming back carrying two steaming mugs of coffee and handing one to my dad. Her voice was a mix of anger and fear.

"Mom I had to try, you even said at dinner that we had to find a way back into the Planes. That no one knew what would happen if we didn't." I looked up at them, begging them to understand.

"She's right Tina love," my father said to my mother, his voice a sigh. He put his arm around her shoulder and pulled her close pressing a kiss to the side of her head, "although it would have been smarter for you to have someone there to anchor you." His gaze landed on me and I fought not to shrink away from the disappointment I saw there.

"I don't think the spell will work with an anchor Dad. It was as if the anchor holds us too tightly to this Plane, not allowing us to travel the Astral Planes."

"You still shouldn't have gone out there alone with no one knowing what you were doing." He scolded gently.

"I know," I sighed, "I didn't think anyone would believe me about hearing the whispers." I admitted.

"I would have," Aiden said. He was leaning against the counter, "you should have said something while we were in the sanctuary yesterday, or even today. You could have said something last night and we could have tried today with the rest of the coven, just in different positions than yesterday. You doing the spell and me anchoring you, or at minimum monitoring you."

The hurt in his voice made me want to cry, he felt like I didn't trust him like we had always trusted each other. "We were both needed to help the others with the ritual today, and we are both exhausted." I tried to argue.

"Then why didn't you wake me up before you went down there? If you were still worn out from yesterday then why did you do this alone?" He demanded angrily, "Didn't you listen to mom? If something happened to you in the Astral Plane, we would have lost you forever." His voice faded with the last sentence.

I opened my mouth to respond but was silenced with a look, "Enough, what's done is done," my father said, his voice even, "McKenna, since you were able to reach the Astral Plane there are a few things you need to know."

"I think we should move into the living room, its further from the stairs and more comfortable." My mother said as she glanced towards the stairs and where the younger kids were all still asleep.

"Of course," my father said with a nod of his head. Mom led the way into the living room, Aiden and I followed with dad at the end. I sat on the same couch that I had fallen asleep on yesterday. My parents sat on either side of me while Aiden leaned against one wall. "Kenna, you know that from your mother's side you are a descendent of Sara Osborn," Dad started, "Sara was from Salem. She fled during the witch trials after the first hanging, her and the other witch families. They each moved to a different part of what is now the United States and started covens much like Sara did here."

"What isn't widely known," my mother picked up the story, "is that before the families left, they locked their major powers into magical items. Each Artifact granted witches one major power. We believe that there are twelve items, Artifacts now, one for each of the twelve major powers. One item from each family, each coven. From reading Sara's Journals and Grimoires, we were able to learn a little bit more about what Sara created. The item that she made, which gives us the power to walk the Planes safely, has come to be known as the Garnet Altar. The Altar along with eleven other blessed items were locked into a protective circle for -"

"Twenty years." I concluded, remembering them saying the last time we were locked out of the astral plane it was for twenty years.

"Yes, at which time each family sent a descendant back to Massachusetts. These descendants were to open the protective circle around the clearing where they had placed these items. Then they returned the powers to all witches and took over guarding the Artifacts." My mother placed her hand on my knee and gave it a light squeeze, "The reason you need to know about our history darling, is because as the only one able to reach the Astral Plane, you must be the one to go to Massachusetts. You have to talk to the Guardians and check on the Altar. You have to find out why it and the other items have stopped giving the major powers."

"Massachusetts?" I looked up at her, I had never left the local small Texan town just down the road from the farm and now I was expected to travel halfway across the country.

"Yes, the Sacred Space is someplace outside of Salem, you will be able to sense it."

"Ok when do we leave?" Aiden asked and I met his eyes with a smile of thanks. As always he had my back, as I had his.

My dad shook his head, "Not you Aiden. Kenna has to go on her own. It's part of the pact signed by the covens centuries ago. When sending witches to the Sacred Space, each coven is only allowed to send one person. It keeps each coven equal and helps to keep the location of the circle safe."

"Alone?" I looked back and forth between them, panic rising in my chest, "But I've never even left home before."

"You will do just fine darling, you are a honorable, smart woman and strong witch. You are the only one who can reach the Planes, so you have to be the one to go. Just trust yourself, you will make the right call," my mother said pulling me into a hug.

"We will send you on your way in the morning," my father said, "Until then we all need to get to bed." He ushered us all out of the living room and up the stairs.

I waited till I heard my parent's door close and then walked over to Aiden's door with a soft knock, "Aiden?"

"I'm awake" his voice was as soft as my own.

I slipped in silently and curled up next to him on his bed, "I'm scared."

"I know, and I wish I could come with you, I hate that I can't. But mom and dad are right you can do this. You are more powerful than you realize, you always have been. I think you are the most powerful of us all. I can't count the number of times that a spell has only worked because I had your powers to draw on. We should have known from the beginning that it would be you who could reach the Planes. You just have to learn to trust yourself, we trust you." I clung to my big brother as I slipped off into a restless sleep.

CHAPTER 10

I WOKE UP TO Aiden shaking my shoulders gently, his voice soft, "Come on squirt, time to go get ready for your big adventure."

I sat up with a yawn and rubbed my eyes, I still felt completely drained and exhausted, "What do I even need to bring?" I asked rubbing the sleep from my eyes.

"I'm sure mom can help you with that." he said. We both made our way downstairs. The kitchen was still empty of our siblings, but mom and dad were already awake and working on breakfast.

"How are you feeling darling?" Mom asked, voice filled with concern as she made her way over to me.

I dropped into the chair I had sat in the night before and looked up at her, "Honestly, I'm terrified that I won't be able to do this, not on my own."

"You can do anything, you know that," my father said walking over to join us and put a comforting hand on my shoulder, "Did you sleep at all last night? You look exhausted." His voice echoed the worry in my mother's eyes. All I could do was shrug in response.

"Come on Kenna, let's go get you packed while your father continues fixing breakfast and Aiden wakes the others." Mom said gently.

"Oh come on," Aiden groaned, "The twins throw things when I try to wake them up."

"You will be fine, you know how to duck," Mom said with a quick grin as she led me back up the stairs. We were silent as we walked down the hall to my room, the door closing as Aiden opened Krista's door. I smiled when I heard her yelp and knew he had flipped the lights on. I was going to miss the chaos of home.

Mom headed straight to my closet and started pulling out all the clothes I had hanging up. I quickly grabbed clothes from the growing pile and changed into a pair of high waisted dark blue jeans and pulled on a thin long sleeved dark green t-shirt. We were silent while we packed most of my clothes into a suitcase, leaving the lighter stuff still hanging. We also packed two outfits in the small duffle bag, Mom explained that we wanted to do this as there was always the slim chance of the suitcase being lost in transit. She then added a set of toiletries to the suitcase, and I added my dagger. Into the duffle bag, I put my journal and a few books that had been sitting unread on my bookcase. I looked around at my room. It had never been cluttered to begin with, but now it felt completely empty, as if I hadn't been living in it for the last eighteen years.

"Mom, what about Zipper?" I asked sitting on my bed, bringing up the first of my many concerns.

"Well, your father and I discussed that. We're going to give you several vials of his sugar water in your carryon bag. When you get to the airport you will need to have him fly over security and meet you on the other side. Once you get through security you will need to keep him in your pocket. First, so that you don't get caught with him. Second, because it's going to be cold in Massachusetts when you land. Much too cold for a small hummingbird like Zipper. Now your connection with him will help some in that regard but you will need to make sure to keep him warm while you are there."

"I understand mom, and I will."

After we were done, we headed back downstairs to join the rest of the family for breakfast. Everyone ate in silence, a heaviness in the air. Dad had told the others that I would be leaving while we had been packing my bags. After breakfast I gave each of my seven siblings a hug, the younger twins holding me tightly, not wanting to let go, their eyes filled with tears. When I slid from their grasp, Aiden and Krista taking them, I hugged my mother tightly, my own eyes filling with tears.

Dad grabbed the suitcase and lifted my duffle bag. I pulled on my boots and grabbed my rarely used purse before we both headed out to his truck.

While Dad loaded the bags into the truck, I cupped my hand for Zipper to land in. "Come on little guy, you get to be lazy for the next few days," I said as I slipped him into my pocket.

"How are you feeling?" Dad asked softly as we pulled from the yard. I looked out at the rest of the coven who had gathered to watch our departure.

"Scared." my voice was more confident than I actually felt.

"If the Goddess didn't believe that you were capable of completing this task she would not have allowed you into the Astral Plane." He was silent for a moment, "If we could send anyone else, you know we would ."

I nodded looking over at him, "I know Daddy." I could see the concern etched into his face.

"There's a cell phone for you in the glove box. It has both the house and Coven numbers programmed in," Leaning forward I opened the small compartment. I pulled out the phone and slipped it into my purse, "Me and your mother want you to check in with us each night please. We will stop on the way to the airport to get you some money. You have one of the coven credit cards as well. Your mother added you to the account first thing this morning. I don't have to tell you to be careful, not to trust too easily."

"I know," I nodded, "it won't be as friendly out there," I stared out the window silently for the rest of the trip. I watched the expanses of farmland dwindle until we were surrounded by tall buildings. I sat silently as my father stopped at the bank and removed several hundred dollars in cash for me. I added a hundred dollars to my wallet, which until now only housed my rarely used license. I then added the credit card he handed to me. The rest of the cash I folded into three bundles and slipped into the duffle bag, hiding them amongst my rolled-up clothes and books. As we got closer to the airport dad started to explain more things to me.

"Your mom is working on making you a hotel reservation now. She will send you a text while you are in the air with the address."

"What about traveling from the airport to the hotel?"

"We will have a driving service waiting for you." He answered, "We don't want you taking any unnecessary risks. Don't worry about looking for the circle today, you have exhausted a lot of your energy. Take the day to recharge and gain your strength." I nodded my agreement and leaned heavier against the door. "they will need to see your ID when you check into security, and also when you check into the hotel. Make sure you keep the money out of sight and only carry a little bit on you at a time."

"Dad, I know I haven't left our small town often, but you and mom did raise me to have common sense." I grinned at him.

He sighed as he pulled into the airport parking lot, "I know Kenna, but we still worry about you." He looked over at me as he put the truck into park.

"I know Dad, and I promise to keep you guys informed with everything I learn."

Dad turned the truck off and we got out. He walked me inside and stood with me as I waited to get my ticket and check my suitcase. He walked with me until we reached the first security check point. There he pulled me into a tight hug where I clung to his shirt. He pressed a kiss to my head, a whispered blessed be our farewell, before I turned to show the agent my ticket and continued deeper into the airport.

As I followed the flow of the crowd to the lines of security I ached for home. I reached the front of the line, toed off my shoes, and opened my bag when requested. While toeing off my shoes, I pulled Zipper from my pocket and set him on the floor, "You need to move unseen Zipper," I whispered to the tiny bird, "be careful and fly as close to the ceiling as you can. I will meet you on the other side with a treat." I stood up and watched as he took off zig zagging through the crowd before flying up the wall to the lofted ceiling.

The tube I was scanned in made me feel claustrophobic and my throat tightened as I thought about the flight ahead. After slipping my shoes back on I grabbed my bag and continued through the airport following the signs to my terminal. Zipper landed on me just out of sight of security check, and I rubbed his delicate head as I slipped him back into my pocket. I checked the time and saw I still had nearly an hour before my plane boarded and decided to stop in one of the gift shops.

I grabbed a bag of chips and a water, grimacing at the inflated costs, before checking out and continuing my way through the crowded airport. I found an empty chair near the terminal and sat down. I dug through my duffle bag and pulled out one of the books. I curled into the seat and opened the book. I was several chapters in when they announced that my flight was ready to board. I was hyper aware, listening to each announcement they made. My head continually jerked up from the book, I was terrified to miss the announcement that my plane was boarding. So when they did finally call my flight I immediately slipped the book into my purse. I stood shouldering my duffle bag and clutched my ticket in my hand.

I was shepherded onto the plane along with the other passengers and I was reminded of when the cows at home were herded into the truck to go to slaughter. The thought caused a shiver to run up my spine and I sent a silent prayer of protection to the Goddess. I found my seat about halfway back, just behind the marked emergency exit, lifted my duffle into the overhead compartment then slid into the seat by the window. It took nearly thirty minutes for everyone to board. Finally, the door closed and the captain's voice came on the PA system and greeted us all.

I pulled the safety pamphlet from the back of the seat and followed along attentively as the flight attendants went over each of the safety measures. When I felt the plane begin to accelerate down the runway, I clutched the arms of my seat my heart speeding up as the plane did. I squeezed my eyes shut as I felt the force of gravity pushing me into the back of the seat, my breath catching in my throat. Once we began to level out I slowly opened my eyes and let out the breath I had been holding.

I was still alive. After a few more minutes I was able to slowly release my hands from the seat. I pulled my book from my purse along with one of Zippers mini vials of sugar water. I slipped the vial into my pocket and continued reading, trying my best to ignore the fact that I was thousands of feet in the air, cut off from nature, and completely powerless. When the plane leveled out I watched as the flight attendants began making their way up and down the aisle. When they reached my seat I was handed a small bag of pretzels and ordered myself a water. I turned to look out the window, watching as the ground moved below us, the houses looking smaller than a penny from this height. That realization made my heart race again and I quickly shut the window cover. I pulled down the tray from the seat back in front of me and opened my book trying to lose myself in the story.

CHAPTER II

I SHIVERED AS I stepped out of the Boston airport and the cold began to seep into my bones. I pulled the heavy down jacket around me as my breath fogged in the air in front of me. I saw the driver in all black holding a sing with my names and headed towards him. When he opened the door I slid into the back with my luggage. I looked out the window watching the strange territory with barren trees and snow-covered ground as it passed by. The ride was only about 30 minutes and I preferred it to the flight I had just come from. I was used to cars. I slipped my hand into my pocket and relaxed further when I felt Zipper snuggle into it.

I pulled up outside of a brick building with a small sign marking it as the hotel mom had made a reservation at for me. I thanked and paid the driver before getting out and walking into the building. I waited at the counter while the lady checked me in and handed me a key to the room I would be staying in. Glancing at the time, I decided to go out for dinner and to get a feel for the town. I would start my search for the Sacred Space in the morning. I tucked the suitcase and duffle bag into the closet, pulling out my small cross body purse. I tucked my wallet, filled with several of the twenties from dad, the cell phone into the purse, and tucked my dagger into my boot.

"Zipper I will be back in a little bit," I said to the small bird flitting around the ceiling, "It's too cold to take you with me," I smiled at him before heading back out of the hotel.

I walked along the streets stopping to read signs that talked about the witch trials. A shiver ran up my spine at the thought of what my ancestors went through. I reached up to my shoulder and touched my hair where Zipper would normally be nestled. I wished I could have brought him but it was too big of a risk to take him out in the cold when just going for dinner and sightseeing.

"Pretty gruesome, isn't it?" a deep voice said from behind me. I turned and felt my breath catch in my throat. Less than a foot behind me was the most handsome man I had ever laid eyes on. He was about half a foot taller than me and had eyes the color of melted chocolate. His hair was a brown so dark it would have looked black without the rays of the setting sun to highlight faint red-brown streaks.

"Um, yeah, the things people do to one another while scared." I replied turning back to the sign.

"You interested in the Witch Trials?" He asked moving to stand beside me, his breath puffing white in the cold air as he spoke.

"Actually, I was just passing through but why pass through Salem and not see what its famous for?" I asked. He was standing close enough to me that I could feel heat radiating from him and I barely suppressed a shiver.

He chuckled softly, "Very true. I'm Gideon by the way," he introduced holding his hand out to me.

"McKenna." I responded placing my cold bare hand in his warm gloved one. As we shook hands, I couldn't help but notice that his hand dwarfed mine, "So Gideon, are you interested in the Trials?" I asked unable to stop the smirk that crossed my lips.

"No, same as you, just passing through and figured I'd see what it was all about." The smile he sent back my way had my heart flipping in my chest. I had never felt like this around anyone and could feel my cheeks heating, "Well McKenna, its freezing out here, and you seem to have forgotten gloves," he grinned, "I was on my way to dinner; would you care to join me?"

I hesitated for a moment and tucked my hands back into my pockets. My father's words of caution echoing in my ears as I smiled, "What a coincidence Gideon, I was also on my way to dinner and wouldn't say no to company." After all, what could going out to dinner hurt?

Within an hour we were sitting in a dimly lit restaurant. A small candle between us.

"So where are you from?" I asked as the waitress set our food down in front of us.

"Depends on what you mean by from," He smiled over the rim of his glass as he sipped the dark amber liquid. "I grew up in New York City. Manhattan to be specific. Though I only really spent the summers there."

"What do you mean you only spent the summer there?"

"I went to Karrow Boarding School. It was about three hours away from home in Manhattan."

"Why so far away? Didn't you miss your family? Your siblings?" I couldn't imagine being away from my family for months at a time.

He shrugged, "It was a good school, and my older brother was there too, so I had family. Not to mention we would go home for the holidays."

"Only two of you, I can't imagine what that's like. I'm the second of eight." I laughed.

"You have seven siblings?" I could hear the shock in his voice and nodded.

"Yes, one older brother and then three younger sisters and three younger brothers," I couldn't help but let my smile go sad as I thought of my family, "I miss them terribly being here. We have never been apart."

"You've never been away from home?"

I shook my head, "Why would I? We had everything we needed right there at home. Have you done a lot of traveling?"

He laughed a little, "You could say that. Senior year of High school I did a foreign exchange to France and completed my

Undergraduate Degree at Oxford University for Law"

"Wow, you have been everywhere, haven't you? What brings you to Salem?"

I watched his face close down just a touch, "Family Obligation. But as soon as it's taken care of I'm heading straight back to School"

"What are you going to school for?"

"I'm finishing up my bachelors in legal studies and come September I'll be starting on my masters in international legal studies."

I looked at him in awe, "You have it all planned out, don't you?"

"What about you McKenna? Why are you here?"

"Learning about the history," I lied quickly, "My parents decided that I needed to experience the world and thought that this would be a good place to start. Truthfully though I can't wait to get back home. I can't imagine being anywhere but home with my family."

He reached out and touched my hand softly, "There's an entire world out there, you shouldn't limit yourself."

"I don't find it limiting and the work we do there is important."

"I understand that farmers are important, but you have seven other siblings to take over the family farm."

"It's more than just a farm. We are a rescue, for both animals and people." It was the only way I could think to explain the work we did in the Astral Planes.

We finished the meal in silence and when the waitress brought the check, he silenced my protest about paying my half and instead covered the whole meal stating that he had been raised to be a gentleman.

As he helped me into my coat, a blush darkened my cheeks again. We found that we were both staying in the same hotel and he offered to walk me back, as it had gotten quite dark outside. We walked back to the hotel talking quietly. Gideon walked me to my room, and we stopped outside of it. A warm smile on his face, he lifted my hand to his lips, and brushed them lightly along the very edge of my knuckles, "It was a pleasure meeting you McKenna." He purred against my skin, his dark eyes on mine.

I felt my chest tighten, cheeks going red. It felt like something had tugged at an area just below my naval. I wet my lips so I could respond, "the pleasure was mine I assure you," My words came out a breathy whisper. I barely recognized my own voice. What was going on with me? When he released my hand, I reached behind me to open the door and slipped inside, heart pounding with excitement.

CHAPTER 12

A S I SLEPT, MY dreams were filled with visions of brown eyes looking at me and the feel of soft lips on my skin. When I woke the next morning, I still felt exhausted. I slipped from the bed yawning and rubbing my eyes. I got into the shower and let the hot water wash away the chills and help wake me up. Getting out I dried off and braided my still wet hair tightly then pulled on a pair of dark jeans and a long-sleeved green T-shirt. I grabbed a dark grey hoodie and my jacket from the closet and slipped my boots on. I sat at the desk and pulled out the phone and called home. The phone rang three times before my mom answered.

"Kenna? Darling are you ok?" Her voice was filled with concern.

"I'm ok mom," I sighed and closed my eyes. Maybe if I pretended hard enough it would be as if I was back home, "Its cold here but other than that I'm ok."

"Have you had any luck finding the Guardians?" Her voice was a little calmer.

"No mom, I looked around town a little yesterday but I didn't see any sign of them. I'm going to leave the hotel after we finish the phone call and start searching. I just wanted to update you"

"Are you sure you are ok Kenna?" I thought back to the night before with Gideon. I ached to get my mother's advice but I knew that it wasn't the time or place.

"I'm sure momma."

"Be safe my daughter, I love you."

"I love you too." I took a deep breath and opened my eyes.

I dropped the phone into my purse and pulled my dagger from under the pillow, where I had slept with it the night before. I slid the dagger into my boot and shrugged the sweater and heavy coat on. I held my hand out to Zipper and tucked him into the coat pocket along with a small vial of his sugar water. I pulled my purse across my body settling it against the opposite hip where Zipper was and I headed out of the room hanging up the do not disturb sign.

As I crossed the lobby, I was glad that I didn't run into Gideon. I didn't want to have to try to get away from him. I needed to start my search for the Sacred Space. I left the hotel and closed my eyes. Taking a deep breath, I lowered the shields my mother had taught me to put up so long ago. I felt a small pulse of something, so faint I nearly missed it. It was to the west, so I headed off in that direction. I pulled my hood up over my head and tucked my hands into my pockets, the sun warming my back.

I walked for hours, following the slowly but steadily beckoning pulse of magic. A few times I felt strong pulses as I passed store fronts and stopped to investigate. A few turned out to be nothing more than a blessed object and a few others were the shop owners inside. I shouldn't have been surprised to meet real witches in Salem, but I was. Though at least two of the shop keepers were shapeshifters not witches, their power was a warm heat that wrapped around me like a Texas summer breeze. I stopped at a small store just as the sun reached its peak in the sky and bought myself a light lunch plus a few small snacks to keep in my purse, and a pair of gloves for my frozen fingers. I wasn't sure how much farther I had to go, but I figured if I hadn't found the sacred space and the Guardians by midnight, I would call a cab back to the hotel. I could take another taxi back to where I had left off in the morning and start searching from there.

At about five o'clock, just as the sky was darkening and my feet and legs began to move past aching towards being numb, I reached the edge of woods. I could feel the pulsing magic calling to me from inside the trees, where nothing should have been. It was still quite distant, and I wasn't sure if I felt confident enough to wander the strange woods alone in the dark.

I stood looking at the woods, chewing on one of the granola bars I had gotten and weighed my options. I could head back to the hotel, call it an early night and possibly run into Gideon again. Or I could go in and finish the task my parents and the Goddess had given me. I peeked into the pocket where Zipper was, "What do you think little buddy?" He chirped at me annoyed, "You're right, might as well get this over with." Sighing I tucked the wrapper into my other pocket and headed into the woods.

CHAPTER 13

AS THE WOODS GREW darker and the beckoning pulse of magic grew, my progress slowed. I wished I had also grabbed a flashlight at the small shop where I had purchased the gloves. The closer I got to the pulsing magic the more noises I could hear, the cracking of branches and crunching of dead leaves. I wasn't sure if it was that there were more animals deeper in the woods or if I was just becoming more paranoid. Just as I was getting ready to turn back, I stumbled to the edge of a clearing and the pulse pounding in my chest and head stopped.

As I stepped into the clearing, so did eleven others. one of which was the dark haired, dark eyed boy who had invaded my dreams. I dropped into a crouch and grabbed the dagger from my boot. I watched as the others all pulled similar small weapons of their own. We all looked at each other over a clearing that was empty save for twelve bodies, who I assumed were the guardians. They lay spread across the ground like dolls discarded by children. Even in the fading light, I could see where their robes were soaked in blood that had then spilled into the ground. Some lay face down in the dirt while others stared blankly at the sky above. My hand began to tremble, and I tightened the grip on my dagger. I felt my stomach churn. Feeling my fear and anxiety, Zipper popped out of my pocket to hover next to my shoulder.

"Ok everyone let's take a deep breath, and calm down" said an older witch, her grey hair pulled up into a bun and a black cat sitting at her heels. I noticed she was the only one who hadn't pulled a weapon of some type and stood hands clasped in front of her.

"The Guardians are dead, the Artifacts are missing, and you want us to be calm?" A dark-haired woman said.

"What she said, anyone here could have been the one to have killed the Guardians." A man said, the large cat next to him emitting a low growl.

"If any of us had killed the Guardians, why would we be here?" A blonde said her voice posh and aloof.

I took a deep breath and slid the dagger through a belt loop at the back of my pants as I stood straight again, "She's right, we all need to take a minute. We aren't each other's enemy," I said, "We should all be working together to find out who killed the Guardians. Then we need to figure out how we can retrieve the Artifacts and return the powers to our covens."

"Whoever took the Artifacts is obviously dangerous to have taken out all twelve guardians. Why would we risk our lives for a couple of ancient relics?" Gideon asked his voice disgusted.

"Because it is why our covens sent us here." I replied turning to face him completely. I felt a mix of betrayal and confusion filling me, "We can't just let our powers be taken from us without a fight. We have to get them back."

"Why, my powers never helped me." A Native looking witch said.

"It's our duty." I replied to her, "not only are our powers part of us but is it our responsibility to use them to keep the universe in balance. "

"The universe hasn't ever done anything for me either." she replied, "I say that if they wanted our powers that badly then we let them have them and we all get on with our lives." I was shocked by the number of others who nodded their heads in agreement.

"We were all sent here because we are the best our covens have," an older gentleman said stepping forward, a motion of his hand keeping the large dog sitting where it was. He wore a heavy leather jacket and large boots with jeans, "It is our obligation to retrieve the items and avenge our fallen brethren."

"What he said," I nodded, "But honestly, my parents entrusted me to come here and check on the Garnet Altar. Since it's not here they will expect me to retrieve it and return the ability to the covens to walk through the Astral Planes. So that is what I am going to do with or without the help of the rest of you. And if you aren't going to step up then after retrieving the Altar I will go in search of the rest of the Artifacts since it is the right thing to do."

"If you go alone, you will get killed. You are too naive to be on your own" Gideon said nearly rolling his eyes. I bristled under his words

"Just because I haven't travelled most of the known world doesn't mean that I can't take care of myself." I growled. I could feel the others in the clearing were watching us in obvious curiosity.

"And who says she will be alone?" A man stepped forward. He was tall with long black hair that he had combed back, and sun kissed skin, "I agree with her. We have to retrieve the artifacts and return the powers to the covens." He turned to me, and said "I'll go with you."

"I'm down, we have to get our powers back." the dark-haired witch said as she too stepped forward.

"I think the rest of us should take care of the dead. Then we need to find and prepare a new Sacred Space for when the items are returned. We can't use this one any longer. It's been tainted by too much death," a man stepped forward, skin dark and voice thick from the south.

"I am not letting her go out without me. She'll get herself killed." Gideon growled. Him bouncing between insulting and protective had my head spinning, but I tried to push it away.

"Great," I said looking at the others, "Now the question is, how are we going to find the Altar and the other Artifacts without our powers?"

"I think I can help." A voice said and we all turned to see the newcomer stepping into the clearing.

CHAPTER 14

GIDEON STEPPED IN FRONT of me, putting himself between me and the newcomer, "And who are you?"

"My name is Malek, I'm a local shifter." he said staying towards the edge of the clearing as the rest of the witches gathered behind Gideon and me. He was tall, with wide shoulders. His hair fell to brush along his collar bone and he had a thick dark beard that covered the lower half of his face.

Rolling my eyes, I stepped around Gideon so I could talk face to face with the shifter, "It's nice to meet you Malek, but how can you help us?"

"I witnessed the murder of your Guardians as you called them. They put up a struggle. I was running in the woods and heard them but couldn't reach the clearing in time to save anyone. I did see the other witches though, and I can follow their scent and their magic. I can help you trace them."

"They were murdered at least three days ago," the biker witch said from just behind me, "why are you still here?"

"My pack has been here since the trials. We knew of this space and of the Guardians, so I knew you would be coming quickly to check on them once the ancient artifacts were removed."

"And how do we know that you and your pack aren't the ones who killed the guardians and took the artifacts?" Gideon asked, voice hostile.

"You don't, but if that were the case why would I have stayed here waiting for you?"

I turned to look at Gideon, "He's right, if he had anything to do with the Guardians death, he wouldn't have stayed here."

"So, what we are just supposed to trust him?"

"Do you have a better way to find the ones who killed the Guardians and get back our powers?" He looked away for a moment and I could see his jaw whitening from clenching his teeth, "I didn't think so." I turned back to Malek, "thank you for the offer of help, we truly do appreciate it. It's too late for us to head out tonight. Would you still be able to help us tomorrow? We can meet you back here in the morning." I said.

"Tomorrow or a week from now, I will not forget the witches' scent. We will be able to find them. Until tomorrow." Then with a nod of his head he turned and melted back into the black shadows of the forest.

"How do you know we can trust him?" Gideon asked.

"I don't," I could hear the exasperation in my own voice, "but honestly we don't know if any of us can trust each other. As I said, he is our best hope." I responded moving my hands to my hips.

"As it is now neither here nor there, I think we should take care of our dead." the dark witch from earlier said, "my name is Jamal by the way."

"McKenna," I said taking the hand he offered, "and while I agree we must honor them. I'll be honest, I'm lost as to what we should do with it being so late." I looked over the fallen Guardians and my stomach clenched again causing Zipper to trumpet nervously.

"For now, I think the best we can do is to lay them respectfully and cover them with cloth. I have some herbs back in my room that I can bring in the morning to bless them with. I feel that the best thing we could do is to bury them here" the older witch with the bun said stepping forward, "my name is Gwendolyn, but please call me Gwen."

"It is nice to meet you Gwen," And with that introduction we set to work.

We laid the twelve dead men and women side by side flat on their backs, arms crossed over their chests, lowering their eye lids respectfully. Many times through the work I had to stop and walk away as I felt my nearly empty stomach rolling from the smell of death. I was constantly wiping my hands on my jeans trying to get rid of the feel of their cold skin under my hands. My arms burned from the constant lifting and carrying of fully-grown people.

"Hey you ok?" Gideon's voice was soft behind me as I leaned heavily on a tree one hand on my stomach as I tried to keep my eyes from filling with tears.

"No, I'm not ok. I'm not sure how so many of you are able to be ok with this." I said turning to look up at him.

"I'm not ok with it," his eyes were as soft in the dark as his voice was as he looked down at me, "And a few of the others have had to walk away once or twice as well. There is no shame in that."

"I'm not ashamed but sickened at the carnage here." I barely knew him but at that moment I wanted to step into him. I wanted to beg him to wrap his arms around me, just to feel warm living flesh against mine.

"We are almost done here and then I will take you back to the hotel, unless you brought a car of your own," His voice was the most unsure I had ever heard it.

"No, I walked."

"We are over fifteen miles from the hotel, you walked here?"

"I didn't have a car and I didn't really know where I was going" I shrugged.

He gave a small laugh, "As soon as we finish, I am taking you back to the hotel and getting you food, you look pale."

"I had been munching on granola bars and fruit on my way here, but I'm not sure I can eat after this." I said. I looked back to where three of the witches were laying the second to last guardian next to his brethren who had already been placed.

"Why don't you take her home," the biker said quietly walking over, "We can handle the last one without the two of you."

"I can stay and help," I protested. I could tell I was one of the youngest in the group and didn't want to be accused of not pulling my weight.

"Lil-one you have been big and tough today, but the paleness of your skin and the darkness under your eyes tell me that you have finished your part in this. Besides, you have a long day ahead of you tomorrow, I will be sending Zander and Adriana along here soon as well."

"Thank you, Randall," Gideon said shaking the gruff biker's hand, "Come on Kenna, at minimum you need to get into the warmth." With a sigh I conceded to his point and we made our way back through the woods.

It took us about forty minutes to make our way back through the woods, Zipper humming along beside us. When we came out there was a sleek silver car waiting in the dark. Gideon opened the door for me and closed it once I slid onto the leather seat. I pulled my purse into my lap and Zipper nestled himself in my hair. I watched as he walked around the front of the car and opened his own door, sliding in behind the wheel. I couldn't stifle a yawn when he turned the car on, and green numbers blazed telling me in was one in the morning.

"You can rest," he said his voice soft, "I won't hurt you."

"Why do I trust you so easily?" I asked blinking my eyes a few times to try to keep them open.

He laughed sharply, "If I could answer that question for myself maybe I could give you an answer. Rest McKenna, we will be to the hotel in about half an hour and we can get you into your room." I watched out the window until I could no longer keep my eyelids open and let them fall heavily.

It seemed like only moments later that Gideon was carefully opening my door and helping me sleepily from the car. I leaned into his warmth only focusing on keeping my feet moving one step at a time. When we got to my room Gideon stopped in front of the door.

"Kenna, where's your key?" he whispered.

"Purse," I murmured. He grabbed my purse and dug through it for a few minutes before pulling the key out. Gideon opened the door, guiding me inside.

"Gideon, I don't want to be alone." My voice was soft and even I could hear the fear in it.

"Let me go to my room and change and I will be back," he said gently, "why don't you get ready for bed in the meantime?" I nodded and watched him walk out of the room, my key in his hand. Zipper tumbled from his spot on my shoulder. He flew off to the small nest on the dresser I had made from towels for him and was fast asleep as soon as his wings stilled. I quickly pulled the clothes off that I was wearing and changed into my pajamas, which were more suited to a winter in Dallas than that of Salem. They were a pair of thin cotton pants and a thin tank top. I had just settled onto the bed when Gideon let himself back into my room. He waited for me to slide under both the blankets and sheet, then turn on my side before crawling in next to me. He laid on top of the sheet, so it stayed between us. Without thought I turned into him, put my head on his chest and closed my eyes, exhaustion carrying me away.

CHAPTER 15

I WOKE WITH A heavy arm around my shoulders holding me against a strong chest. My eyes flew open. What had I done last night? My mind and heart began to race as I thought back over the night before, "Good Morning, Kenna." Gideon's voice was soft and as I started to sit up, he let his arm fall from my shoulders to my waist.

"We should get ready to go; we don't know how long we will be traveling," I said sliding to sit on the edge of the bed, I could feel my cheeks flushing bright red. What the hell was I thinking asking him to stay with me last night?

"Hey," I felt the bed dip behind me and then I felt his hands gentle on my shoulders, "are you ok?" He pulled me back against his chest, hands kneading my tense shoulders.

"I shouldn't have asked you to stay here last night," I said looking out the window into the morning light.

"And why not?" I could hear the hurt in his voice as his hands stilled but didn't leave my shoulders.

"Because I barely know you," I had to bite back the tears.

"I think that we both saw horrible things last night that we are not used to, and neither of us wanted to be alone." He slid farther onto the bed to sit next to me. He tucked an arm around my shoulders using his other hand to tilt my chin up to look at him. "Nothing happened between us. Nothing other than innocent comfort," I searched his dark eyes with mine. I found nothing but compassion in them and nodded. "Now let's go get dressed and pack up. We can check out and grab breakfast before we head back to the clearing to meet the shifter."

"Sounds good, though we should stop on the way to the clearing and get supplies, and the shifter's name is Malek." I waited until he nodded, after rolling his eyes, and smiled at him," Good then I will see you in an hour in the lobby?" he nodded and I smiled as he stood and brushed his lips over my forehead before heading toward the door.

Once the door clicked closed behind him, I stood and pulled a new vial of sugar water out for Zipper and woke him from his nest. Once he was circling the room I headed toward the shower. I let the hot water wash over me. I kept my eyes open and my back to the spray, not wanting to chance seeing the slaughtered bodies of the Guardians now that Gideon had left me.

I washed and dried quickly, opting to blow dry my hair and leave it down before dressing in another pair of dark jeans and long sleeved dark brown t-shirt. I tucked the clothes from the last two days into a bag and put them into one side of the suitcase. As I repacked, I reorganized both the suitcase and the duffle bag along with my purse, so everything was more easily accessible. Pulling the cell phone from my purse I sat at the small desk and dialed home, Zipper landing on my shoulder.

"Hello?" Mom's voice made my heart squeeze.

"Momma." I had to hold back the tears.

"Kenna, love, are you ok?"

"Momma," I stopped and took a deep breath, "The Guardians are dead, and the artifacts are gone." the words rushed from my mouth. She pulled the phone away from her ear and I heard her call my father over.

"Kenna, darling, please start from the beginning. Tell us what has happened." Her voice was calm and soft.

I took a deep cleansing breath, trying to distance myself from the events of the night before and told her what had happened. I pulled my feet up onto the chair, my knees against my chest, and rested my chin on them.

"Only four of you are going to look for the Garnet Altar? What are the rest going to do? Are they going to look for the other artifacts?" my father asked.

"Well, not everyone is convinced looking for the artifacts is the right thing to do," I confessed. I thought about Gideon's displeasure at my insistence to retrieve the artifacts. "But the others are going to work on setting up a new secure location for the Sacred Space for when we retrieve the artifacts" I answered.

"Do you need one of us, or maybe Aiden, to join you?" My mother asked. I thought about it for a moment. It had only been two nights and I missed my family terribly. However, I knew that I had to finish this without them here, besides I had Gideon with me. I trusted him, despite just meeting him and his resistance to finding the artifacts.

"No, I think this is something I have to finish on my own. I will find the Garnet Altar and the other artifacts." I vowed, "I will return all of the covens' powers to them."

"We know you will Kenna, and we are so proud of you" my father's voice echoed with pride, "we must go now and inform the coven of your news. Be safe my daughter, Blessed Be."

"Blessed Be." I hung up the phone and closed my eyes, tears burning. I had to make sure that I was deserving of their pride. Taking another deep grounding breath, I stood to finish getting ready to leave. I put my boots on and tucked my dagger back into them before I pulled my coat on. I grabbed my bags and headed toward the door; Zipper snuggled into my chest.

I was just finishing checking out of the room when Gideon stepped up to the counter next to me. He waited for me to finish. Placing a hand on the small of my back, he quietly asked me to wait for him. I smiled up at him as I stepped aside so he could check out of his room.

When he finished checking out, he took my duffle bag from me. He chuckled when I tried to argue, "My mother would kill me if she found out I let you carry your own bag when I was perfectly capable."

"You know your car isn't going to fit everyone." I said looking at the shiny sportster.

"I already called the rental company. We're going to stop there after breakfast and swap it out for an SUV. Then we will have plenty of room for everyone, and for the Altar when we find it." He said placing our bags in the trunk.

"Well, well, well haven't you just thought of everything?" I teased laughing.

He grinned at me as he closed the trunk, "ready to head to breakfast?"

"Let's go," I turned to head to the passenger door when he grabbed my hand.

"Lets walk," he grinned as he fit our hands together. I smiled and let my fingers entwine with his as we walked through the streets of Salem. We stopped outside what looked to be a small bistro. We walked into the small building waited for the maître'd' to seat us. We sat at a small table for two and I was thankful for the menu as I tried to hide a yawn.

"You can rest while we drive," he said softly, and I looked up to see him watching me.

"We don't know how long the drive will be, and I'm not sure I'll be able to rest with so many people around us." I kept my voice quiet.

"I won't let anything hurt you, you know."

The irritation from the night before came back in a rush. "Yes, you made it clear last night that the only reason you are coming with is to keep me safe as you seem to feel that I am inept at the task."

"I never said that."

"No, I believe your words were naïve."

"Where is this coming from?"

"I called my parents this morning" I said. I thought over the phone call I had made that morning, "I don't think they believe I can do this alone. They offered to join me or send my older brother to help me. I know to everyone I seem to be the wrong person to be doing this, but there must be a reason why I was the one able to reach the Astral Plane when no one else could. I have to be able to do this."

I watched him think over my words, his eyes on mine, "It's not that I don't think you can do this. As you've pointed out, I barely know you, but these people took out the Guardians. According to my parents, the Guardians were highly trained. I mean they would have to be with what they protected, and they were slaughtered. So, whoever took the artifacts must be extremely dangerous. I know you think that getting the artifacts back is now your mission in life, but I don't think that these stupid items are worth your life or mine. I also don't think any of us are as well trained as the guardians were, and now we are powerless."

We paused our conversation as the waitress came over to take our order. Gideon ordered a platter of eggs over easy, toast and sausage with a cup of coffee. I ordered peaches and cream crepes with hot chocolate to drink while ignoring Gideon's look of amusement. Once she walked away, I turned back to him voice still lowered to avoid outsiders hearing our conversation, "What those artifacts gave us make us what we are. Without our magic we lose who we are as a people."

"Would being like normal humans really be that bad?" He reached out and took my hand in his, "Kenna, look around, we are in a town famous for their history of killing people accused of being us. They aren't the only ones in history to do so either. If the world found out that we existed, I couldn't even imagine the outcome." His chest rose as he took a deep breath, "Who knows maybe we would be lucky in this new modern era where being Wiccan is looked at as cool and hip. But it is just as likely that we would be killed using the elements we work with; hung, burned, drowned, or crushed."

I saw the fear in his eyes and squeezed the hand that held mine, "there are more of us now than there were back then Gideon. I'm not saying start a war, but we could protect ourselves better. Also, just because we get our powers back doesn't mean we have to come out to the world, it just means we keep what makes us who we are. I grew up going in and out of the Astral Planes, and honestly, I ache to be back there. I miss tending to the animals and crops, balancing the universe, and keeping the peace."

"I will help you retrieve the artifacts, Kenna. Not because I think we need them and not because I don't think you can do it, but because I want to make sure that you stay safe." he took another breath looking out of the small window we sat in front of before bringing his dark eyes back to mine, "and because I want to be by your side while you do what you believe needs to be done."

"Thank you, Gideon, it means a lot to me." As the conversation came to an end the waitress came back with our food and we both ate quietly. The silence tense, not due to a strain between us, but in preparation of what was to come.

When we had finished eating, and Gideon had once again paid the bill, we walked back to the hotel. Once there Gideon led me over to the car and held the door open as I slid inside. I grinned at him as he closed the door, and I watched him walk around the front of the car. I blushed as I caught myself watching how his jeans clung to his back side. I looked out the window to hide my reddening cheeks as he pulled away from the hotel. I watched Salem pass by the windows as he drove through the town. Gideon stopped a few blocks from the rental and opened the back window. His raven darted out the window and took flight.

"Do you have a familiar? We aren't supposed to have animals in the vehicles." He said as he rolled the window back up to cut off the arctic air that had drifted into the Car.

I nodded, "But he's not used to this type of cold. I can keep him in my pocket like he has been most of the day."

"What is he?"

I pulled Zipper from my pocket and the small bird woke with a rapid shake of his head, it worried me how often he had been sleeping the last few days while we were in Salem, "This is Zipper."

I watched Gideons face as shock, then confusion and finally disbelief washed over it all before he quickly reschooled his face into a blank mask and nodded, "Your pocket it is, just please keep him out of sight," The rest of the drive was silent, but it seemed to hold more tension in it.

When we got to the rental lot I stayed in the car, which Gideon kept running, while he went in to make the trade. When he came back out there was a sales guy with him. I watched as they went over to a pickup truck. Gideon shook his head as he talked to the guy who then lead him to a large SUV. They shook hands and then the guy slid into the driver's seat while Gideon walked back over to me in the small sportster. I went to open my door and Gideon shook his head.

He opened the driver side door and grabbed his phone from where it had been laying, "Stay in here till I get the bags switched over. By then the SUV should be warmed up."

"I won't die from a little cold Gideon."

"I know you won't, but you are going to be out in the cold soon enough. Besides, the little guy in your pocket will do better in here," He added lowering his voice.

I rolled my eyes but stayed in the car. He had a point about Zipper. I watched in the side mirror as Gideon moved the bags into the back of the large SUV. When I heard the trunk close, I opened my door and slipped from the warmth of the car and into the brisk cold air outside. I snagged my purse from the floorboard and closed the door. "We good to go?" I asked walking back to the men.

"Just have to sign a few papers," Gideon smiled, "Do you have everything?" I nodded holding up my purse, "Then go get settled and I'll be back out in a moment." He squeezed my hand softly and smiled at me. I felt a flutter in my stomach and nodded heading around to the passenger seat. I curled myself into the seat and reached in to run a finger over Zippers head, letting myself find comfort in the small bird. After a few minutes Gideon slid into the driver seat and we were off.

"We need to stop at a store before we reach the woods." I said as he pulled onto the street.

"What do you need?"

"We won't be reaching the clearing until nearly noon. We won't have helped the others with any of the graves. The least we can do is bring them lunch, but also we can get lunch for those going with us and ourselves while we are on the road."

"You seriously want to feed all of them?" he looked at me in disbelief.

"Yes, my mother would be ashamed if I didn't at least try to."

He nodded, "Then off to a store we will go." I smiled at him before turning back to look back out the window.

When we got to the woods, we moved to the back of the truck. I pulled out the dog bed, hand warmers and blanket. I used them to form a small nest that would stay heated even with the car off for an extended period of time. We pulled one of the two large coolers out from the back and closed the hatch, leaving Zipper and Gideon's Raven familiar, Onyx, in the car nestled into the heated nest. We made our way through the woods with Gideon carrying the cooler, despite me offering to help. We reached the clearing just as the sun was peaking overhead. The others were all gathered there.

At the edge of the clearing opposite of where we entered, I could see where they had already dug the first three graves for the Guardians. As we entered, I watched as four of the guys lowered the first Guardian to their final resting place. The older witch, Gwen knelt next to another body her hands moving a little above the body a bundle of sage burning in her hand.

"So glad you could join us." Adriana said from where she lounged against a tree.

"I stopped to get us a larger vehicle for travel and supplies for the road," Gideon replied in an uninterested tone as he set the cooler onto the ground.

"What did you bring?" one of the others asked. She was a tall woman of what looked to be native descent. Her hair fell into a straight sheet of black to her lower back as she huddled into her dark red jacket.

"Lunch," I said with a smile, "we had to stop and get supplies as Gideon said and I felt bad not being here with everyone first thing this morning so I figured we could at least bring you food."

"That was very kind of you." Gwen said softly as she stood from next to the body, she had finished blessing.

"How's it going?" Gideon asked from next to me.

"It would be going faster if it wasn't January and the ground wasn't frozen," The tall Hispanic male said as the group walked over from the first grave, "Alec by the way, not sure if we had a chance to meet earlier." He said pulling off his glove and holding his hand out towards Gideon.

"Nice to meet you, names Gideon." I watched as they shook hands, "I know a heat spell. With all of us here we may be able to gather enough magic to thaw the ground."

"What do we have to do?" Gwen said standing from next to the body she had just finished blessing.

Gideon shrugged, "it's a fairly simple spell. My brother and I used to do it while we waited for our driver to pick us up from school. I think that we can tweak it to defrost the ground." He turned and set the cooler against one of the trees. He turned and looked at the clearing and the people spread throughout it, "if we all line the clearing, about ten feet apart from each other to form a circle, I think this will work."

I move to down the line of trees to stand to Gideon's left, Alec moved to stand to his right. The taller man from the night before, Zander I think was his name, stood on my other side. Next to him was the older gentleman Randall, then Gwen. Adrianna Stood next to Gwen with a blonde next to her. Then a tall middle-aged man whose skin had seen more sun than my own, then the Native American who had asked about the cooler, an Asian witch who stood nearly a head shorter than the rest of us, and finally the very tall very dark black southern man stood on the other side of Alec.

Gideon crouched down and held his hands out to his sides, palms down, "like this" he said softly. he watched as we all imitated him and I felt that spark of power ripple around us. The woods rustled and suddenly animals joined us, including Onyx and Zipper. I watched as the familiars took their place to the right of their owners, Zipper hovering in the air between Gideon and I. With each animal that joined the circle the power grew until my hair lifted in the breeze that we created. Gideons voice was soft but firm as he spoke, "I call upon the Spirit Keepers of the south, Guardians of Fire, we ask you for your warmth. Spirit Keepers of the south, bring to me your heat. Guardians of Fire, lend us your flames. Three times asked, three times granted so mote it be." I felt the wind that whipped around us begin to heat and looked over to meet his eyes, he gave a short nod.

Again he repeated the spell, and this time I added my voice to his, "We call upon the Spirit Keepers of the south, Guardians of Fire, we ask you for your warmth. Spirit Keepers of the south, bring to me your heat. Guardians of Fire, lend us your flames. Three times asked, three times granted so mote it be." Again, the heat around us grew and again we repeated the chant, this time with Zander and Alec joining us. We repeated the spell four more times and as each person joined us the heat around us rose until the snow from the tree tops fell down like rain evaporating before it could touch us. I could feel the ground beneath my feet softening and as the last word slipped from my lips I stood back up with the others and felt rejuvenated.

"That was amazing." I breathed grinning at Gideon. He smirked back at me while Jamal and the cowboy looking witch each grabbed shovels and began to dig.

"This is going to make things a hundred times better" Jamal called over with a grin, "thanks."

Gideon nodded, "so where are we supposed to be bringing these artifacts when we find them?"

"What about in New Orleans?" Jamal said coming back over to join us, "Its full of the paranormal and there are lay lines that we can pull power from."

"It would be like hiding in plain sight," The Native American witch said joining us again, "I'm Misty by the way." She smiled.

"It's not a bad idea." I looked at the others.

"It's settled then, we will find a place in New Orleans," Alec said.

"Are we ready to go then?" Malek asked, dropping from a tree only feet from me and Gideon.

"Depends, do you know where we are going to find these murdering bastards?" Gideon crossed his arms facing the shifter.

"I know that they went north." Malek said, " I can track them as we go, their magic leaves a distinct... smell."

"Well then let's head north and see just how well you can track this smell." Zander said coming over, a good-natured smile on his face.

"You kids stay safe and we will let you know when we have found a new place to settle." Randall said also coming over to join us.

We said our goodbyes to the others and gave a last short blessing over the dead. The five of us made our way back through the woods to where Gideon had left the shiny black SUV, we had traded the silver sports car for.

CHAPTER 16

WE ALL SAT AROUND the back of the SUV to eat the lunches we had picked up.

"So what's the plan?" Adriana asked as she tossed a small hunk of her sandwich to the large black shepherd by her side.

"Malek will give us directions to where he senses who ever stole the artifacts, Gideon will drive us there, and we will get back the artifacts." I said.

"Just like that uh?" Zander asked.

"I hope so" I stood and dusted off my hands, "I have no idea what to expect though to be honest. As Gideon said yesterday, whoever these people are, they are dangerous. They have to be to have taken out the Guardians without a major fight."

"We ready to go?" Gideon asked looking around to see that everyone had finished their sandwiches.

"Let's go try not to die." Adriana said patting the dog's head.

"Where is everyone sitting?" Zander asked.

"You three in the back, McKenna and me upfront." Gideon said.

I shook my head, "It makes more sense for Malek to be upfront as he will be the one telling you where to go. Besides the back is going to be cramped with three people back there and it makes more sense for the smallest of us to be two of the people back there."

Despite Gideon's protests I sat in the back with Zander and Adriana, leaving the passenger seat to Malek. The tension in the car was thick as we drove.

After the first several times of Malek telling Gideon he needed to turn or change direction in a place that there was no road, we decided to stop for an atlas and for dinner. We stopped at a small steak house on the side of the highway just over the border into New Hampshire and all headed inside. I squeezed into a booth between Gideon and Zander while Adriana and Malek took the booth on the other side of the table. The waiter came and took our drink order sending a flirty smile toward Gideon. As she walked away, I shifted just the smallest bit closer to him.

"So Malek, may I ask what type of shifter you are?" I asked quietly making sure we wouldn't be overheard. Zander snickered quietly and shook his head next to me.

"A big one," he answered with a sheepish grin. "Sorry but it's not something we really talk about. Each animal has its own weakness so maintaining that secret keeps us safe."

I nodded and smiled at him, "Of course, I was just curious is all." I turned to Zander next to me, causing me to lean against Gideon a little more. He lifted his arm allowing me to settle in next to him, "Where are you from Zander?"

"Vegas. So, this cold snow crap is killing me." he said with a grin just as the waiter returned with our drinks. We paused our conversation and waited as she set the drinks down and began to take our order.

Once she had walked away again I grinned at Zander, "I feel you about the cold. I was born and raised in Texas, the first step out from the airport was definitely a shock to me." I looked across the table, "What about you Adriana?"

"Please call me Ade, Adriana makes me think I'm in trouble." She grinned, "And I'm from Chicago, so this cold is right on target for us. Though I'll admit the wind back home is ten times worse." From there we fell into easy conversation about where each of us was from, with me curled up under Gideon's warm protective arm. When the waitress returned with our food the conversation died off as we ate. When we were finished eating, Gideon took the check as soon as it had hit the table. Once she had taken it back along with his shiny black credit card, I turned to him.

"How much do I owe you?"

"Don't worry about it, the coven can cover it."

"Thank you but you didn't have to do that." My voice was soft as the waitress handed him back the card and receipt. We all stood and Gideon held my coat out for me. Once he had helped me with my coat, causing my cheeks to burn red again, we all headed back out to the car. This time Zander slid into the front and Malek sat in back with me and Ade. Malek would tell me where we needed to go. Ade and I would then work out which streets Gideon would need to take using the atlas and let him know the route to take.

About an hour later we hit the boundaries of a state forest and Gideon pulled the car to the side of the road.

"They are in there." Malek said.

"How far?" Adriana asked.

"I don't know, but not very. I can smell the death rot on them." There was a faint growl to Malek's voice, and it sent a shiver up my spine.

"It's too late for us to go hiking through strange woods tonight," Gideon said. "We can find a hotel close by and start out first thing in the morning." No one disagreed and Zander began to use his phone to look for a place for us all to stay. About ten minutes down the road we found a small motel.

When we all walked in the young girl behind the counter looked up, "How many rooms?"

"I want my own room," Ade said her voice firm.

"Same." Zander and Malek echoed.

"Four rooms." Gideon said before I could add in my opinion. I glared up at him, "I don't trust them enough. I am not leaving you alone." He whispered into my ear as the others all formed a line to check into rooms.

When it was our turn the girl didn't look up from the computer, "Name, ID, Credit Card, and one bed or two?" she asked.

I stepped in front of Gideon answering before he could, "McKenna Pomengale and two beds please," I said handing over my ID and credit Card. The girl tapped on the keyboard a few times looking down at my ID as she did. She swiped the card through the reader and handed both cards back to me.

"Just need a few signatures," she smiled up brightly as she handed me a few papers. I looked through and signed them as I had at the previous hotel and handed them back to her, "Thanks, I put you guys in the last room by the others." She grinned and handed me the key cards. I thanked her and we headed back out to meet the others by the car. We grabbed our bags from the back along with the three familiars. Zipper and Onyx hovered around Gideon and me, while Ade's big shepherd jumped out to stand at her side.

"What's his name?" Zander asked ducking his head towards the big dog.

Ade grinned, "Capone." I couldn't help the soft laugh that slipped from my lips and heard the same sound from Zander and Malek, even Gideon was grinning when I looked over at him. Closing up the car we headed toward our rooms, me and Zander sticking close to the building in hopes it would keep us a little warmer.

When the door closed behind me and Gideon, he dropped his bags on the first bed, the one closest to the door. I rolled my eyes but continued in farther to where I assumed the bathroom was.

"I'm going to call home and get ready for bed." I said as I walked into the room.

"I'll change out here." His voice was soft behind me. I didn't look back as I closed the door. I set my bag down on the sink counter and pulled the phone out of my purse. As the phone began to ring, I sat on the edge of the toilet.

"Kenna?" Aiden's voice filled my ear.

"Aiden," my heart ached for home hearing my big brother's voice.

"What's going on?"

"Goddess I wish you were here." I said softly.

"Are you ok? Do I need to get mom and dad to let me come up there?"

I thought about it. Was I ok? I had no idea, "I'm alright," I lied to him. I didn't know how to explain the problems we were having. I was not going to tell him about Gideon no matter how badly I wanted another person's opinion on things, "We traced things to New Hampshire. We have a rough idea of where the first artifact is. I'm not sure if it's the Garnet Altar or not but I will let you guys know as soon as we find it. We are going to go after it tomorrow."

"Why not today?"

"It's too late. We only have an approximate location not an exact location and none of us feel like searching through strange woods at night."

I could see him nodding his head like he always did, "Ok that makes sense. What are the other witches like?"

I had to think about it, "They are different. Like each one is completely different. Some of them act like they don't even want to get the powers back, which I can't understand."

"Well watch your back, ok? And let me know if you need me, I will find a way to make mom and dad let me come help."

"I will," I smiled at the reassurance, "I should be getting to bed. We will be heading out early tomorrow morning."

"Take care of yourself sis."

"I will, promise." I hung up the phone and tucked it back into my purse. I pulled the pajamas out of the bag and changed into them quickly. I brushed out my curls before pulling them into a tight French braid. Once my dirty clothes and brush were tucked back into my bag I turned to the sink and quickly brushed my teeth and washed my face. I left my small toiletry bag out on the sink and turned to leave.

I hesitated at the door. Gideon was out there. Why was I suddenly nervous? We had shared a bed last night and I hadn't been nervous. Tonight, we were only sharing a room. It was nothing. I took a deep breath and lifted my chin, shoulders rolling back, and opened the door and walked out. My breath slipped out between parted lips when I saw Gideon sitting on the end of the far bed. He was in the same dark pajama pants that he had worn this morning and a white t-shirt that was tight along his shoulders. He stood and smiled at me, with a small black case in his hand. I quickly stepped out of his way my gaze falling to the floor.

Gideon walked past me to the bathroom, hesitating at my side for just a second. I waited but he didn't say anything, just continued past me into the bathroom. When I heard the door close, I moved to the bed and set my bags down on the bed. I pulled out a container of sugar water and the small fleece nest I had made for Zipper. I set both on top of the dresser in front of the TV and closed my bags back up. I moved the bags to the floor between the wall and the bed, and pulled the covers back to climb into the bed. I had just settled into the pillows when Gideon opened the bathroom door and came back out. I turned onto my side to keep myself from watching his every move. He stopped in front of the TV for a few seconds, running his hand over Onyx's head, before moving to double check the locks of the door and turn off the lights. I listened to him slip into his own bed in the sudden dark and closed my eyes. I listened to his deep and even breathing, letting it lull me to sleep.

I woke up to the sun slowly filling the room, through the now open window.

"Morning," Gideon's voice was soft, and I found him sitting at the small table and smiling at me, "I was going to let you sleep a little longer. The others will be here in about an hour and a half and food will be delivered at about the same time." I nodded and slipped from the bed.

"I'm going to take a shower really quick." I said softly grabbing my bag from the floor.

"Kenna."

"What?" I looked over my shoulder at him and couldn't quite understand the look on his face.

"Is everything ok?"

"Yeah. Why wouldn't it be?" I stepped into the safety of the bathroom and closed the door like a shield between us. I didn't understand the feelings that being around Gideon caused, but I knew that I needed to push them aside and get the job done. I needed to focus not on the boy in the other room but on finding the artifacts and getting back to my family. I turned the shower on and pulled my hair free from the braid while the water warmed. I stepped in and let myself get lost in the hot water, doing my best to ignore the fact that there was a near stranger in the other room. When I felt like I could no longer hide in the shower I stepped out and quickly dried off, pulling my hair back tightly while it was still wet and twisting it to the top of my head. I pulled on a pair of jeans and a long-sleeved shirt, this one a dark ruby nearly the same color as my hair. I slipped my dagger into my boot and could feel the whispers of its magic wrap its way up and around my leg and felt instantly comforted. I made sure everything was put away in the duffle bag with enough room for Zippers stuff and walked back out.

I added more sugar water to Zippers feeding jar and nuzzled the little bird as he flitted up to my face, "Its ok boy." I whispered and smiled at him, "I'm ok."

Zipper had just settled onto one of the bright plastic red flowers around the glass jar when there was a knock at the door. Onyx let out a soft squawk and rose in the air before flying over to land on Gideon's shoulder. Gideon moved and opened the door to the other three. Zander came in first, his eyes flicking between me and Gideon with a look of concern in them. Behind him was Malek and Ade with Capone bringing up the rear. I sat at the head of my bed and leaned against the headboard, legs crossed and watched the others. Gideon and Malek sat at the small table, both of their shoulders tight with the tension of being in the same small area once again. Ade flopped onto the bed Gideon had slept in and the large dog jumped up and laid with his head on her knee. Zander nudged the TV back as far as he could and sat on the dresser next to where Zipper was feeding. I watched as a small lizard climbed from his pocket and down his arm to investigate the fleece nest.

"Who's that?" I asked nodding towards the lizard who was now exploring the nest.

Zander grinned and picked the small green animal back up, "This curious chameleon is Dazzle." A moment later there was a second knock on the door and Gideon answered it again, this time handing the gentleman on the other side several bills and taking bags and a drink carrier from him. We all sat and ate the breakfast sandwiches in silence. When we were done the others went back to their rooms and gathered their bags before we met back at the car. The ride back to the woods was short and the car was filled with a heavy silence. Gideon turned the car off and we all got out, Adriana's black Shepherd at her heels, with Onyx and Zipper taking to the sky. Zander lifted Dazzle onto his shoulder.

I looked to Malek, "Are you going to shift before we go in?"

"No, I'm hoping that we won't need me in my animal form," he said solemnly. I nodded in understanding.

Gideon stopped me on the side of the truck as the others all got their gear out of the back of the car, "Promise me you won't risk your life for whatever artifact it is that they have."

"I can't guarantee that," I said looking up at him. "I promised my parents that I would do whatever it took to get the Altar back."

"I don't think they would want you to give up your life McKenna." his voice a growl to match Malek's.

"I won't purposely get myself killed. I don't want to die," I said feeling my irritation rising. His eyes searched over my face. In the end he nodded, and we moved to the back of the SUV. I grabbed the new backpack Gideon had insisted I get before we had left Salem and slung it onto my back over the winter coat.

"Here," Zander said holding a dozen or so small vials out to me and Gideon.

"What are these?" I asked eyeing them.

"Whoever we are about to face are apparently dangerous, and we have lost the powers we are used to using to defend ourselves. What we haven't lost is our abilities to make potions to replicate some of those powers and a few that we didn't originally have." He said with a shrug, "The Seers Circle Coven is best known for our seeing ability; premonitions, crystal balls, Tarot and Runes readings. Nothing that inspires fear in our enemies, so we started working on defensive potions. I made these last night after Malek told us what we were facing. Blue will immobilize, pink will create a circle of fire, red explodes, and black, well black is acid."

"And your coven has been making these without telling the rest for how long?" Gideon asked distrust coloring his voice. He took the small vials and rolled them in his palm as I divided mine between pockets. I crouched down and pulled my dagger and its sheath from my boot and relocated it to the small of my back.

"We ready?" Adriana asked, swinging her own backpack on. She rested her hand on the big black dog's head next to her.

"Yeah, I think we are good to go." I said looking over the crowd. We all set off into the woods, Malek in the lead.

CHAPTER 17

THE WOODS HID THE tight rolling hills that we had to make our way through. More times than once, Gideon had to catch me before I tripped over hidden roots and fallen branches. The hike was slow and tiring. We watched the sun moving across the sky through the barren tree branches above us. After about three hours, we could hear faint chanting echoing through the woods around us. Our pace slowed even more as we attempted to silence our movements.

Holding up a hand, Malek halted our movement forward. I looked questioningly at Gideon who gave me a small reassuring smile and reached down to squeeze my hand. As he did the others moved off into the woods and I could see that the woods thinned and cleared about twenty feet in front of us. Our fingers still entwined Gideon held me where we were until there was a short cry of a raven overhead. Onyx was giving us the all clear.

"Remember, whatever they have isn't worth your life." Gideon whispered into my ear. I nodded as we stepped into the clearing. Two women and a man stood in a circle and at the center I could see a small table made of aged wood. My heart sped, they had the Garnet Altar.

"Step away from the Altar." I ordered pulling my dagger from behind my back as Zipper came to hover over my shoulder. The three turned to face me and Gideon and I saw the others emerge from the woods forming a larger circle around the three.

"Now why would we do that?" one of the women asked her gaze narrowing on me.

"Because you stole it. It's not yours and neither is the power that it grants." Gideon responded, and I felt a flicker of annoyance as he pulled the attention to himself. Even now his instinct was to protect me, to not trust me to take care of myself.

"You don't deserve the powers." the man sneered.

"But murderers do?" I challenged.

"We only killed them because they tried to stop us from taking what was rightfully ours," the third woman scoffed.

"Lies," a growl rang through the clearing. I looked across at Malek and could have sworn I saw him vibrating, "the man you killed begged for mercy. You laughed as you killed him." I heard my blood rage in my ears at his words.

The first woman laughed, "he was a blundering old fool and deserved no mercy."

With a vicious growl I watched as Malek took three running steps before launching himself into the air. What landed on the woman was a giant brown bear. Her shrill scream was like some sort of signal, as suddenly the small clearing burst into motion. The two other witches who were standing by the Altar turned with flames flicking in their hands.

I saw a flash of red out of the corner of my eye flying through the air toward the two witches. There was a sound of glass shattering as the potion vial hit the earth a moment before the ground in front of the male witch exploded in a shower of dirt and rock. Suddenly there was a ball of fire hurtling toward me. Then a hard shove into my side sent me to the ground, landing on all fours, as a wave of heat passed over me. There was a pained cry from behind me and turning quickly, I saw Gideon lying face down on the ground. Rage washed over me as I screamed his name and crawled toward him. A clink of glass caught my attention and plunging my hands into my pocket, I pulled out the vials of potions. Looking at the rainbow of vials in my hand, the rage burning inside me turned cold. I threw a blue vial first and watched it shatter at the feet of the last witch still standing, freezing them in place. I was only faintly aware of the sounds of tearing flesh behind them as Malek removed the remaining female witch's head from her body.

I glanced back down at Gideon, tears still burning in my eyes. The tightness in my chest released the smallest fraction when I saw his back rise and fall, signaling that he was still breathing. I knew my eyes were cold when I looked back up at the two frozen witches. I slid a pink vial into the hand that held the red and black vials and stood.

"Get the Altar and move away," I ordered. I didn't recognize my own voice, the tone colder than the air around me. A quick glance in my direction and neither Adriana nor Zander argued. They quickly moved to the Altar and lifted it moving it off to the side, in the direction of the SUV that we would need to get it back to. Malek padded over to stand next to me. His front paws were tipped in red leaving bloody paw prints, his muzzle dripping red spots into the snow. Standing next to me, even on all fours, his shoulder was higher than my head. I threw all three potions at once.

"No!" Zander shouted when he saw the mix of colors fly into the air, but it was too late. They landed together with a shatter of glass. I watched as a ring of fire exploded around the three witches. I heard the screams of the two once frozen witches as the acid flames ate them alive, filling the air with the stench of burning flesh.

I fell back to my knees next to Gideon and moved to roll him over, "Wait!" Zander slid to his knees next to us, "make sure you aren't rolling him over onto the potion vials. We don't need any more explosions." I nodded and tucked my hand into both back pockets. Finding them clear I rolled him onto his back. Zipper and Onyx landed on the other side of him. His eyes went wide, as he gasped in pain, his hands reached up to clutch my arm. The left side of his blue down jacket had melted to his skin, showing the large red and black burn that was about the size of a bowling ball. Zander quickly and efficiently checked his front pockets but also came up empty handed.

I looked up at the others, "He's hurt we have to get him to a healer."

"We have to meet up with the others, one of them must be a healer still from the Serenity Circle Coven." Adriana said moving to kneel on the other side of Gideon. I felt a soft nudge and looked up into Malek's large brown bear eyes.

"W-would, can you carry him back to the car?" I asked setting my hand against his warm furred leg. He nodded his large head once before laying himself flat on the ground next to us. It took all three of us to move Gideon from the ground onto Malek's large furred back. The entire time he made short pained sounds through clenched teeth.

"I won't be able to stay up by myself." he gritted out, and I noticed he seemed to be paler than a few moments ago and his skin had a sheen of sweat. Malek gently nudged me with his muzzle. I took that as the ok and climbed onto his furred back, Gideon leaned into me heavily and I wrapped my arms around his chest. Malek lurched to his feet with the others on either side of us. I glanced down and my vision swam as panic rushed over me from the height. I closed my eyes and took a deep breath before tucking my face against Gideon's neck. Adriana and Zander then lifted the Garnet Altar and began to lead the way back to the SUV, with Zipper and Onyx circling around us and Capone bringing up the rear.

CHAPTER 18

THE WALK BACK TO the car was longer than it took for us to get to the clearing. Zander and Adriana needed frequent breaks due to the weight of the altar. I was constantly asking Malek to stop as the jostling of his gait was causing Gideon to make pained sounds. When we finally got back to the SUV Malek laid back down. I slid from his back, Zander coming over to help me pull Gideon down. As soon as his weight left Malek's back he began the transformation of turning back to human. Adriana opened the back door of the SUV and we slid Gideon onto the back seat. Adriana started the car as Malek and Zander loaded the altar into the back and arranged our packs around it.

Zander held up a hand full of vials, "Well these weren't going to do him a whole lot of good sitting in the car." He looked at me as he slipped the vials into his bag.

"I'll talk to him about it once we know he's going to be ok." I said looking up at him. I slid into the back of the vehicle and knelt by Gideon's head.

"Will he be ok?" Malek asked from the door. I looked up from where I knelt on the floorboards softly stroking Gideon's sweat-soaked hair.

"He has to be." I said quietly looking up at the shifter. "Thank you for your help Malek, we wouldn't have found them without you."

"I'm just sorry that one of yours was hurt." There was worry in his eyes as he looked at Gideon, "I must be off, back to my pack in Massachusetts. I wish you all safe and speedy travels."

"The same to you. My coven owes you for your help."

"Think nothing of it, my clan does not condone murderers and thieves." With that he shut the door just as Zander slid in behind the wheel with Adriana in the passenger seat.

Zander reached back and handed me his cell phone, "Talk to Gwen. We have a two to three-day trip to make it to where they have relocated."

"I don't think Gideon will last that long." I said taking the phone, "Not without a healer."

"Which is why you need to talk to Gwen. She's going to tell you what to do," he said turning the car on and pulling away. "We are going to find a hotel to stay the night. We can work on him there."

I put the phone to my ear, hands shaking just a little. "Hello?"

Gwen's voice filled my ear, brisk and authoritative, "McKenna, I am going to give you a list of supplies you will need to get. Most can be found at a grocery store or a health food store. You may also need to make a stop at a pharmacy. You need to start by keeping him hydrated, get lots and lots of water. You are also going to need tweezers, a lot of washcloths, antibacterial soap, aloe gel, gauze, tape and plastic wrap. Also get him some ibuprofen for the pain. Once you have all the supplies call me back and I will talk you through what you need to do."

"Ok I'll call as soon as we have what we need and find a place to do this." I said typing the list into my phone as she gave it to me.

"I would suggest somewhere out of the way where you won't be disturbed. You won't be able to do anything for the pain, and this will be painful. You don't want to be anywhere where someone may call the cops on you. Which also means you can't go to a hospital; they will have too many questions."

"Ok we will see what we can find. I don't want to hurt him," I said softly.

"I know hon, but you don't have a choice. If this is not done the wound will get worse and he may not live if it gets infected." her voice was gentle now.

I took a deep breath and closed my eyes, "ok." I hung up the phone. I sent the shopping list to Ade as I settled onto the floor of the SUV, my head resting on the seat next to Gideon's.

"We will stop at the next town and get the supplies. Then we will drive a bit farther and find a hotel for the night. I think it would be best if you do the cleaning and bandaging here in the car. That way if he yells no one will hear and call the cops." Ade said. I just nodded eyes still closed.

I felt the car stop about an hour later and opened my eyes again. "Ade is running in to get the supplies we can from here and there are a few more stores we can check after this one." Zander said gently, "We'll get him all fixed up." Ade came out twenty minutes later with a cart full of supplies. Zander got out of the car and headed to the back to help her make room in the crowded trunk.

"I found everything we need here." She said sliding into the car.

We drove for a bit longer until Zander found us an empty rest area. He parked as far from the small building as he could and turned the overhead dome light on. We laid out all the supplies and called Gwen back.

"You need warm water to start." She said her voice calm, "and you are going to want to have the washcloths ready for use. Get them soaking in the warm water and antibacterial soap" We opened two bottles of water and poured them into a stainless-steel bowl. We nestled the bowl inside of a slightly larger bowl lined with hand warmers. We added in the antibacterial soap and soaked the cloths in them. I started by unzipping and removing Gideon's coat. Adriana had been thoughtful enough to get him a new one. He let out a pained groan as I peeled the melted fabric away from the wound.

"To start you will need to remove any debris from the wound. This is going to hurt him, but if you don't, he could get an infection. Use the tweezers to remove any large pieces of debris and dead skin."

"This is going to hurt Gideon, I'm so sorry" I whispered into his ear.

"I'll hold down his shoulders." Zander said. He stood in the open door by Gideon's head. "My friend you are going to want to bite down on this," He placed his belt, folded in half, between Gideon's teeth.

"And I'll hold his legs," Adriana finished as she opened the other door, "can you do this?"

"I don't have a choice," I whispered. I pulled on the plastic gloves and one of the pairs of tweezers from their package. I closed my eyes and took a deep breath. Opening my eyes again I began to use the tweezers to pull away and remove the melted plastic and blackened chunks of flesh. By the time I reached the center of the burn Gideon was screaming through the teeth he had clenched over Zander's belt. I pulled the last piece that I could see and dropped the tweezers into the sandwich bag that I had next to me. I pulled my gloves off and brushed a hand over Gideons forehead, "Do you need a break?"

He spit the belt out panting, "Just finish it Kenna, the sooner we get it done the better." I bit my lip and nodded as Zander placed the belt back between his teeth.

"Gwen what's next?" I asked.

"Wipe the wound down with the washcloths, you can't be overly gentle with this. You have to make sure the wound is fully clean. When you do this, it is going to hurt him a lot, but it is a must. Once the wound is clean and fully debrided, cover it in the pure aloe gel, make sure it's a thick layer, and cover it in plastic wrap and then use tape to hold it down. You are going to need to repeat this process twice a day until you get here."

"Is that all we have to do?" I asked as I grabbed one of the small plastic garbage bags and placed it next to me on the floor.

"Yes. That should hold him over until you get him down here. At which point I have several salves and poultices that I can use to help speed his recovery." I nodded to Ade who took the phone and said our goodbyes to Gwen before hanging up. I slipped on a new pair of gloves and grabbed one of the soaked washcloths. I squeezed it out and began to scrub at the wound. As Gideon began to scream again, tears began to stream down my face. I went through six washcloths, squeezing them out before using them on the wound. I dropped them into the bag, before grabbing the next one. Finally, I grabbed the bottle of aloe and popped the cap, pouring the cool gel over the wound and spreading it in a thick layer.

"I need him to sit up," I whispered as I pulled the cling wrap from the box. Zander helped to sit him up with Ade pulling gently on his shoulders. I began to wrap the thin plastic around Gideon's torso, not stopping until I had used the whole roll. I grabbed the roll of duct tape from the bag and covered the plastic wrap making sure that there was none sticking to his skin. Once the entirety of the wrapping was covered, I pushed Zander to the side and scrambled from the car. I tripped over the curb and fell onto all fours into the wet grass and heaved bile onto the lawn. I felt a soft hand on my shoulder and looked up into Zander's concerned face.

"He's asking for you, are you ok?"

I nodded and stood shakily, "I'll be ok."

"We need to get going. We still haven't found a hotel" he said as he helped me back to the SUV. I opened the door, glad to see the mess that had been made cleaning his wounds had been cleaned up. He was sitting up in the back seat now, head tilted back eyes closed. I slid in tentatively next to him, worried about hurting him despite knowing the wound was on the other side.

"Come here," he said softly lifting one arm to the back of the seat. I moved closer tucking myself into his side. I rested my hand on his chest well above the burns. "I'll be ok, you did exactly what you needed to do." His voice was rough from the screaming he had done. I closed my eyes and rested my head on his shoulder as Zander started the car and headed back to the Interstate.

I woke up as Zander pulled into the parking lot of a hotel. I waited in the car with Ade and

Gideon as Zander ran in to get us a room. He came back out a few minutes later and opened the back door.

"They have one room left on the first floor," he said handing Ade a key card over her seat, "Room 120, it's a bit of a ways down the hall but it's the best we can do." he said as he helped Gideon and then me from the car, "you guys go in I'll bring in the bags."

I helped Gideon from the car and the three of us slowly made our way into the hotel. Adriana held the door open for us and Gideon settled onto the first bed with a pained groan.

"Do you need anything?" I asked perching myself on the edge of the bed.

"Just sleep," he whispered hoarsely.

"I have to go and update my coven, I'll be back as soon as I can." I said giving his hand a squeeze. I pulled the small cellphone from my bag and walked into the bathroom bringing pajamas with me. Sitting on the edge of the white bathtub I dialed home.

"Kenna, how are you?" My mother answered.

"I have the altar," I said closing my eyes.

"Oh, sweetheart that's amazing news," she sighed, and I could nearly touch the relief in her voice.

"I also killed a dark one," my voice trembled. I squeezed my free hand into a fist trying to steady myself, "and burned two others."

"Were you hurt?"

"Not me, but one of the other witches was, his name is Gideon. We are treating him and are on our way down to the new sacred space."

"Where at hon?"

"I don't know for sure. I'll come home as soon as I can. I love you guys," I said before hanging up the phone and turning it off. I changed into my pajamas and headed back out into the main room. Zander had joined us with the rest of the bags and had pulled out the foldout bed from the couch. Adriana slipped in past me into the bathroom with a small bag tucked under her arm. I stood next to the bed and looked down at Gideon. His face almost peaceful in his sleep. Carefully, I got onto the bed next to him, resting my head on his chest when he slid his arm over my shoulder.

We all woke up before the sun had risen and headed out. Gideon leaned heavily against me while Zander went and checked us all out. Ade took most of the bags for us as we made our way out to the car. I helped Gideon into the back seat before moving around to help Ade get the bags and familiars all settled into the back. We gathered the supplies we needed and put them into a bag in the back seat. When Zander came out I slid in back with Gideon and Ade took the passenger seat again.

We found another rest area and pulled in. We assumed the same positions as the night before. This time Gideon reached up, wincing as the wound stretched and tugged, and gripped the back of Zander's legs. It took less time with the tweezers as I only had to pull little pieces of charred skin from near the edges. Again, Gideon screamed into the belt as I began to scrub at the open raw wound, and I had to fight back the tears. He sat up with little help when I was finished, Ade dumped the water and bagged the washcloths as I covered the wound in aloe and wrapped him in plastic wrap and gauze. Once he had his shirt down and coat back on the other two got back into the car and we got back on the road.

We stopped about an hour later at a small roadside café for breakfast. I had to urge Gideon to eat the eggs he had ordered and even then, he only ate about half the food. When we had all finished, we headed back out to the car.

"Do you want me to drive for a bit?" Ade asked as she fed Capone several slices of bacon.

"If you want to, that works." Zander tossed the keys to her and we all got back in. I curled up against Gideon's side with a yawn. I felt him slide his fingers through my hair just as Ade pulled back onto the Interstate and let my eyes drift closed.

When I woke up we were pulling off into a gas station. "How close are we?" I asked sitting up and yawning with a stretch.

"It's gonna take us about another two days." Ade said turning to look back at us, "Gwen called and gave us the address while you guys were sleeping. Unless you guys have a reason not to, the rest of us have all agreed that we need to keep the new place a secret from everyone."

"By everyone you mean?"

"Everyone. We don't tell anyone outside of the twelve of us."

"What about the new guardians?" Gideon asked.

"Don't you get it? We are the guardians now. We are the strongest of our covens, we are now the guardians." Ade's words hit me and I sat back the breath rushing from me.

"Does this mean that we can't go home?"

"I don't think so. I think that as long as we all agree not to tell anyone where the new space is then there should be no reason not to go back home from time to time."

Gideon wrapped an arm around me and pulled me into his side while I sat in stunned silence to process what I had learned. I wasn't going home. I would no longer have Aiden just across the hall, I wouldn't be able to listen to the twins on either side of me. I could feel my eyes filling with tears as my throat tightened with the effort not to cry. I looked back up to Ade, "Do you have family to go back to?"

"Just my Coven," she turned and looked out the front window, "I grew up in the foster system. When I turned eighteen the Wind City Coven reached out to me and recruited me. I have been with them ever since." Zander got back in the car as she finished.

"What about you Zander? Any family to get back to?" I was fighting to keep the tears from falling. If I focused on the others I couldn't dwell on myself and maybe I wouldn't start to sob like a baby.

He looked over to Ade, "You told them I take it?" She nodded as she pulled back out onto the road, "No I don't have any reason to go back to the coven; I do hate the fact that I'm giving up my apartment less than a mile from the strip though." He grinned back at us.

The rest of the drive was silent. I leaned against Gideon's side and pulled my feet onto the seat as I looked out the window and the tears began to slowly and silently slide down my cheeks. Had I known that I would never again be going home for good would I have still tried to reach the Planes?

We stopped at a steakhouse for dinner, Zander insisting that Gideon needed something high in iron to help him heal. Again, it took me pushing for him to eat and he still barely ate half of his meal. I looked worriedly across the table at Ade and Zander, they both met my eye and shook their heads.

"Gideon?"

"Hmm?" He had his head tilted up against the back of the chair, his eyes closed.

"Are you ok?"

"I have a giant hole in my side, so no I'm not ok."

"I know what's wrong, but you have barely eaten the last two meals. You need to eat if you are going to heal." I tried to keep my voice even and not plead with him.

"Eating means other things, things I don't want to deal with while I have a gaping hole in my side." His voice was just barely above a whisper. It took me a few moments to realize what he meant, and I felt my cheeks flame red. I just nodded and leaned in against his good side, I felt him turn and press his lips to the top of my head, "Also, what we need to do again in about an hour is going to hurt and I don't want to have a full stomach for that pain."

"Ok, I'll stop nagging you. At least until we get to New Orleans, once Gwen finishes with you I am going to require you to eat a full meal, no stopping."

"Deal." He chuckled softly.

That night we found another rest stop and another hotel to stay in. This time we were able to get two rooms, though they were conjoined. I curled up with Gideon in one room and let myself drift off into a restless sleep, his pained screams echoing in my ears.

The next day we found a pancake place near the hotel and stopped. I looked down at the large stack of pancakes in front of me but couldn't bring myself to even pick at it.

"Are you ok?" Ade's voice was soft.

I looked up and saw three pairs of worried eyes looking at me, "No I am not ok. In less than an hour I am going to have to once again cause Gideon excruciating pain while you two hold him still. So no, I am not ok." I stood and walked away from the table. I walked out into the bright Alabama sun. I wrapped my arms around myself and leaned against the truck. I heard the soft tapping on the glass and opened the door enough for Zipper to flit out and zoom around my head before settling himself on my chest.

"Do you want me to do the wound treatment this morning?" Zander voice came from feet away from me.

"Who's going to hold him down?" I looked up at the taller and older witch, "I don't have the same physical strength you do."

"Last night I barely had to hold him down at all. I know it doesn't seem like it but it does get a little better with each cleaning. Stand by his head, let him hold onto you, and I can do this last cleaning. We will be in New Orleans by nightfall and Gwen can take over." His voice was gentle.

"I feel like a coward," I whispered and looked up at the morning sky to try to keep the tears that had filled my eyes from falling.

"You are anything but a coward. You are what? Nineteen?"

"Eighteen," I corrected still not looking at him.

"Eighteen and you traveled across the country, alone. Helped to bury dead bodies, bullied a bunch of strangers into doing the right thing, fought three dark, powerful witches, and now for the last two days you have been taking care of the man you care about by causing him extreme pain. McKenna, you are the farthest thing from a coward I have ever met, and I have met a lot of people. You don't have to do this. No one will blame you if you need a break."

"I'll blame me."

"Well, you need to learn to give yourself a break. Let me handle this last one, you can be the concerned girlfriend and hold his hand."

"He's not my boyfriend."

"Only because you met in the middle of a crisis." He laughed and pulled me into a sideway hug, "Don't fool yourself kid, he took a fireball for you. If you think when all is said and done, he will let you walk away, you have another thing coming."

"We ready to go?" Ade's voice rang out across the parking lot. I looked over to see her and Gideon walking towards us, him leaning heavily against her.

"As soon as you get to the car we can head out." Zander grinned at them. When they got there we all got into what had become our standard seats, Zander driving, Ade in the passenger seat, and Gideon and me cuddled in the back seat.

We drove for a few hours before we started checking the rest stops to find one with little to no people. As we had discussed, I stood at Gideon's head and pressed down on his shoulders while Zander scrubbed his wound clean. Gideon screamed into the belt gag, but his shoulders never pushed up against my hands. I wasn't sure if this was normal or if he was wasting strength to stay still under my hands. I hoped that it wasn't the latter. When Zander put the last washcloth into a bag and tied it closed, I brushed my hand over Gideon's sweat soaked hair while he laid on the seat panting. Zander and Ade cleaned up the supplies used and tucked them into the back. Ade put Capone and the birds back into the vehicle, we had decided to let them roam while we worked on Gideon now that we were in warmer weather.

The rest of the drive to New Orleans I leaned against the door, Gideon's head in my lap while I ran my fingers through his short cut hair.

CHAPTER 19

THE HOUSE WE PULLED up outside of looked like an old Victorian mansion, rising high above us with lights flickering in several of the windows. As we parked the SUV the front door opened and I watched as the others poured out of the house, two of them carried what looked like a stretcher. They opened the back door and I slid out the other side. Jamal and Edwin, I think that was the tall tanned man's name, slid the stretcher onto the back seat and helped Gideon lay on it. They strapped him in and Onyx settled on his chest as they pulled him out of the car and carried him into the house, Gwen and Randall on their heels.

I watched them go and moved to the back of the truck with the others. The tall native looking witch was helping Ade to pull the bags from the back. I watched Zander and a tall heavily muscled Hispanic pull the Altar from the back of the truck and carry it toward the house.

"The garnets, where are the garnets?" The blonde witch who stood on the curb asked as they passed her.

"We don't know." I said shouldering my bag and reaching for Gideon's.

"Here let me help with that." The tiny Asian witch said.

"Eris shut the hell up." The native witch said as she picked up Zanders bags and headed toward the house, "if you are just going to stand there and not help with anything then you don't get to make comments."

Ade tossed the keys to the blonde who caught them with a startled expression, "here sugar, make yourself useful and go park the SUV." The blonde, Eris, made a huffing noise and strode to the SUV's driver side door and got in slamming it closed.

"Ignore her," the Asian said as we followed the others into the house, "She is always like this, it's nothing personal to either of you. Though she got worse once we realized we would all be staying here indefinitely. I'm Esmeralda, or Esme, by the way, not sure if we got a chance to introduce ourselves at the clearing and even if we did it sounds like you guys had a hell of a week."

"Thanks Esme," I smiled over at her.

"Alec is the one who helped, Zander right?" I nodded, "He helped Zander carry in the Altar. Randall went with the others to help Gwen; they seem to speak the same shorthand. Jamal and Edwin are the ones who were carrying him and that is Misty helping with the other bags."

"Thanks for that." I smiled at her, "I was trying to remember everyone and just couldn't." We had stopped inside a large foyer, and it was gorgeous with a staircase to the right that seemed to wrap up and around.

"There are three floors and the attic," Misty said stopping at the bottom of the staircase, "the main floor has two large sitting rooms, a huge dining room and kitchen. There is also a half bath down here. The next two floors have three bedrooms and two bathrooms each. There was another tiny room just off the attic but we all decided it was a good idea for Gwen to have a small work shop for her medicine."

"That's only six rooms, where is everyone sleeping?" Ade asked.

"We have had to double up, though the Princess demanded her own room." Misty rolled her eyes. "There are two rooms left. Esme and I share a room, Ed and Alec, Jamal and Randall, and Gwen set up a small sleeping area in her shop."

"And where is the princess's room?" Ade asked, a grin stretching her lips.

"Why?"

"Because I am not sharing a room with Zander, and I doubt Gideon is going to let Kenna sleep anywhere but by him. He seems to think it is his responsibility to keep her safe." I felt my cheeks flame red.

"It's not like that." I mumbled.

"Girl, don't be embarrassed," Ade bumped her hip against mine, "enjoy having the hot ones attention on you!"

"He is pretty good looking in that tall dark and handsome way isn't he," Esme grinned.

"Like the tall dark and good lookin' do ya?" Jamal's southern voice drawled from the landing just above us.

"Wouldn't you like to know?" She grinned back at him, her voice teasing. I was starting to think me and Gideon weren't the only ones who were developing feelings for one another.

"McKenna, Gideon is asking for you, but Zander and Alec want you to come upstairs and help with the Altar." He said, his eyes and voice going a little more serious.

"What are they expecting me to do? I am too tired to try any type of spell tonight."

"I think they just want your opinion on placement," his voice was gentle now.

"Let's go get yours and Gideon's stuff put in the room and you can check on him before you go deal with the magic." Esme said, voice just as gentle. I nodded and followed her up the stairs.

Misty led Ade up one more floor to the other rooms. Gideon's room, and my room too it seemed, was on the first floor up and to the immediate left when you hit the hallway that was the second landing. Gideon still laid on the stretcher but it had been placed on a high table so that Gwen could sit on a stool and comfortably work on his wound. He had been stripped of his top and shoes and was only in his jeans now. I dropped my bags next to the door and walked over to the side opposite from Gwen.

"How are you doing?" I asked softly as he took my hand.

"I would say fine, but I am starting to think that what she had you guys do for the past three days was in preparation for her own torture," he grit his teeth and his back bowed at the end of the sentence. His hand convulsed and tightened around mine as his eyes closed.

"What are you doing?" I asked looking over to Gwen and wondered if my face was as panicked as my voice.

"I am drawing the heat from the wound." Her voice was soft and she never looked up from her work. She had a table next to her covered in jars and a large bowl of water with piles of rags on either side of them. "Part of why he is in so much pain is that it is still burning, much like a sunburn continues to burn for hours to days later. Once I have the burning stopped, I can begin the healing. This isn't going to be fast, without my magic it is still going to take a day or two to fully heal him and even then, the likelihood of him having a scar is high."

"I don't care about scars; I just want him to not hurt. He took the fireball that was meant for me."

"Then he saved you." Randall said as he took the pile of dirty rags from the table and placed them in a bag. "With the height difference alone, that wound would have been a hundred times worse than it is for him."

"It would have hit her head on," Gideon gritted out.

"A heart blow," Gwen's voice was soft and filled with horror, "They meant to kill you Kenna." I just nodded and looked down at Gideon through the tears that filled my eyes. He had saved me.

"I have to run up and check on the Altar, will you be ok?"

"Yeah, I'll be alright." His voice was hoarse as he talked and he never opened his eyes.

I leaned down and pressed my lips to his forehead before pulling my hand reluctantly from his and left the room. Eris was just hitting the top of the stairs as I closed the door behind me. I fell into step behind her as she headed up the next flight and followed her up to the next large landing, neither of us speaking a word. When she peeled off to go to what I assumed would be her room, I continued up the next set of steps.

I had just hit the first small landing when I heard her voice screech out behind me, "What are you doing in my room?" I shook my head and laughed. I had a feeling that Ade was going to enjoy messing with the spoiled little blonde. I continued up, the sound of their voices fading behind me. At the top of the stairs, which had seemed to have become even steeper, was a door. I knocked once and opened the door. The room was a perfect octagon. The room was maybe ten feet wide from each of the eight sides. In the center of the room was a large rug, about six feet in diameter. Along the walls there were boxes piled in almost every corner. The Altar sat just inside the door to the left.

I walked in and admired the intricately woven black and white rug in the middle of the room. The center was filled with a large pentagram which had been encircled in runes. "It's gorgeous work" I whispered.

"Misty made it on the way here. It will protect those casting in the space, while also amplifying the powers of the items within," Alec said from where he was leaning against the wall.

"Jamal said you guys needed me?"

"We need to know where the best place is to put the Altar." Zander answered.

"The point of the star should point north and the Altar should be centered in the room." I said.

"The door is north," Alec said. Him and Zander moved to lift the old heavy wooden table so the point of the star was aimed toward the door.

"Do we have a chalk marker?" I asked.

"Why?"

"Once we have gotten the Altar to work, we will need to create Portals here. Once we have Portals to the Astral Planes, then all the other Covens should be able to get their portals back online as well. I want to mark where each plane should go." Alec handed me a large marker and I grabbed a step stool by where it leaned against one of the walls. I started on the wall to my immediate left and using the step stool and one hand to balance myself, I stood on tiptoes and wrote out each plane as high up on the wall as I could, moving to the next wall in line for each Plane. When I had finished, I handed the marker back to Alec, "I'm going to head downstairs and wait to hear about Gideon." My voice was soft as I left.

I leaned against the wall next to the bedroom door with my head back and eyes closed as I listened to Gideon's pained moans with sporadic screams through the wall. Gwen's soft voice tried to soothe him as did Randall's rough one.

"Do you think the altar will work without the gems?" Eris demanded.

"Honestly I'm not sure, and until I know Gideon is well I don't care." I said opening my eyes just enough to see her standing at the bottom of the stairs arms crossed over her chest.

"We will try it in the morning Eris," Jamal said coming up the lower stairs, his thick southern accent washing over us, "Once McKenna has had time to rest and recharge. We also need to get the rest of the protections activated."

"You are not in charge here Jamal," she glared at him before turning to me, "and if the altar doesn't work, then what?" she demanded.

"Then I will hunt down all seven of the stones until we are walking the astral planes again," I said slowly sliding down the wall until I was sitting, one leg straight the other one bent. I wrapped my arms around my bent leg and let my head fall forward.

"Why should we trust you to do anything? You couldn't even bring us the full Altar and you nearly got one of us killed."

"Eris, that's enough." Jamal cut in again.

"No, she's right. Gideon got hurt protecting me, and we have no assurances that the Altar will work. But Eris, what have you done to help the covens?" I glared up at her, "What have you done to help anyone? From what I've heard you have done nothing but whine and make everyone's lives harder. So until you are willing to put your obviously privileged self on the line, just keep your mouth shut." I didn't recognize the growl in my own voice.

Eris looked at me, her mouth opened in surprise, then her eyes turned hot and she looked to Jamal, "Aren't you going to say anything to her?"

"Like you said Eris, I'm not in charge here. May I suggest you stop pissing people off though?" She let out a squeal of anger and turned with a flip of her hair to storm off down the stairs. Just then there was a guttural moan from inside the room.

"He will be ok," Jamal assured me as he slid down the wall to sit next to me, "Gwen's talents in healing are legendary."

I looked over at him. I knew my eyes would be as weary as my voice, "Do you know what it's like to use tweezers to slowly pull burnt or dead flesh from an open wound before scrubbing over that wound with a washcloth? In some places I think I could see bone just below the muscle," I swallowed back the bile that threatened to rise, closing my eyes.

"No, I don't. What I do know is that he would rather have gone through what you had to do to him, than the pain of an infection." He reached over and set his hand on my shoulder giving it a squeeze. "You did good. It wasn't easy, but you did good." His southern voice was soft.

The door opened and Randall poked his head out, "Kenna, Gideon's asking for you."

I scrambled to my feet, Jamal slipping a hand under my arm to help me up as he too stood. I walked into the bedroom and paused.

Gideon had been moved to a full-sized bed and was nearly as pale as the white sheet that was pulled up to just below his shoulder. Gwen sat on her small stool at the head of the bed and was placing a cool cloth over his forehead.

"Kenna," his voice was hoarse, but I heard my name clear enough when he said it. I rushed over and fell to my knees at his side.

"I'm here Gideon" I said taking his hand.

"Come here hon," he said pulling on my hand.

"You're hurt." I said knowing what lay in front of me under the blanket.

"Not as much as he was." The weariness in Gwen's voice shocked me. Gently she pulled away the sheet and I bit back a gasp when I saw what looked now like only a severe rug burn where the gaping wound had been only a few hours earlier, "we will need to do at least one more treatment but he will be in significantly less pain than he has been the last few days."

Again, Gideon pulled on my arm and this time I let him pull me onto the bed. Still not trusting the wound I slid over him and curled between him and the wall. I laid my head on his chest and we both let out an exhausted sigh as he pulled me closer with an arm around my shoulders. I opened my eyes as the light in the room went out and saw Gwen and Randall standing in the open door.

"I need to test the altar," I said softly, starting to sit up.

"Not tonight." Gideon whispered into my hair, "We are both exhausted, and I need you here with me."

"Gideon we have to know if it will work."

"We all need rest. The Altar can wait a day or two," Randall said and gently closed the door.

I woke the next morning with Gideon's arm heavy over my shoulders and his heart beating strong under my ear. I sat up slowly and looked down at him. He had regained his color through the night and the shadows under his eyes had nearly faded completely. I wanted to sigh in relief.

"Good morning." He said softly, still not opening his eyes.

"Good morning," I laid back down letting my head once again rest over his strongly beating heart, "how are you feeling?"

"Surprisingly well." He chuckled softly before pressing his lips gently to the top of my head, "we should get up, I'm sure the others will be waiting for us."

I nodded and let him help me sit up. I watched as he sat up, scanning his face for any hint of pain or discomfort, but he showed none. We both changed into fresh clothes with our backs to each other.

"You ready?" he asked, voice muffled telling me he had yet to turn back around. I tugged my shirt into place and turned to face him.

"All ready." I said with a smile. He turned to face me a soft smile pulling on his lips. He reached out and tucked my hand into his, leading me toward the door.

We could hear voices coming from somewhere lower in the house and to our left, so we headed towards them. Soon we found ourselves in a dining room. There was a large rectangular wood table spanning the center of the room surrounded by the others from the clearing and piled high with food. There were two seats still empty along the table, so we headed towards them.

"How are you feeling Gideon?" Gwen asked as he sat after tucking my chair in under me.

"Much better, thank you." He smiled at her and I knew that he had turned on the full charm by the flush that tinted her cheeks.

Gwen smiled at him, "You are welcome. Though like I said yesterday, we need to do one more session today," Gideon nodded his agreement to her.

"Well now that we are all whole again, can we talk about the fact that the altar upstairs isn't?" Eris asked.

"Eris, can you chill for one minute?" Ade snapped from where she sat, "While you were here playing Suzy home maker some of us were out there risking our lives and getting injured."

"I'm just saying, we need to know what we are dealing with is all," Eris snapped back, "and yes we have all heard how the hero Gideon nearly died to save the precious Kenna."

"Wow Eris, can you sound more jealous?" Misty cocked her head to the side, "and when were you planning on leaving to find your coven's artifact?"

"I am not jealous of that child. And I am waiting on orders from my coven," she huffed lifting her nose.

"Daddy can't tell you what to do forever little girl," Alec's deep voice said

"That's enough, we all are going to need to learn to get along," Randall said from where he sat at the head of the table.

I took a deep breath. I looked down at the full plate Gideon set in front of me, no longer hungry, "Listen guys, I don't know if it will work or not without the gemstones," I answered. It was the true unasked question, "but Eris is right the only way to truly know is to try it."

"After you eat." Gideon said setting a hand on my knee under the table and giving it a squeeze.

I rolled my eyes and muttered, "yes dad." I heard him growl. I grinned and dug into the plate of food.

"And rest up some more," Gwen added, her tone of voice made me ache for my mother, "we all know that natural magic is more draining and you are going to need all of your strength.

The small talk around the table resumed. I noticed that besides the four of us who had been out getting the altar everyone had seemed to already be forming into a tight group. Even Eris seemed to get along with the rest when she wanted to. Gideon slid his arm over the back of my chair as we ate. When I finished, I leaned into his side with a sigh. I smiled when I felt him brush his lips over the top of my head.

"What did you want to do today?" he said softly.

"I need to call home and update them, I won't tell them where we are, but I need to let them know that I am safe. And about us becoming the next Guardians.

"We were all talking about heading down to the French Quarter and checking out some of the Wiccan shops, you guys should join us," Esme smiled at me and Ade.

"Do we really think they are real?" Ade asked as she pulled apart strips of bacon and tossed them to Capone and a few of the other larger Familiars.

Misty shrugged, "we have no clue. But since we are going to be here for a while we all figured we needed to figure where to get supplies."

"Because y'all didn't have enough delivered already?" Ed asked but not like he expected an answer.

"We only ordered the bare minimum for basic spell work, not to mention that we may need something odd on short notice and not want to go hunting it down online and paying expedited shipping." Misty reasoned and I watched as Edwin lifted his hands into a defensive posture.

"Ok I give, I will leave the shopping to the ladies."

"You guys could start working on the raised garden beds out back," Gwen said softly, "having access to fresh herbs is never a bad thing."

"Don't worry, we will get your flower beds put up," Randall grinned.

CHAPTER 20

AFTER BREAKFAST I CALLED and left a voicemail for the family to give them an update and then I grabbed my purse and headed downstairs to meet the other girls, minus Gwen, who said she was going to oversee the building of the garden beds, and Eris who made a comment along the lines of its not a boutique so why? As we were leaving Gideon and Zander also headed out, saying that they needed to return the rental, and Gideon talked about getting himself a small car.

We had the guys drop us off in the Quarter on their way to turn in the car, and promised that we would get a taxi, not an Uber, back to the house. There were so many stores to check out that after a few hours we found a small pub and all sat down for lunch. I learned that we were all second born in our family, and I made a mental note to look into that, wondering if it was the same for the others. I also learned that there had been talk of adding to the house, a library downstairs and another three rooms to each floor, to bring the total to twelve rooms so everyone could have their own.

"But I guess we only really need eleven huh?" Ade grinned at me.

"What do you mean?"

"You and Gideon. He's got it bad for you girl."

"I don't know what you are talking about." I looked down at my plate and could feel my cheeks begin to burn.

"Kenna have you ever dated anyone?" Misty asked, her voice a soft curiosity.

I shrugged, "no not really."

"Ok then take it from us. He likes you. And if you let him, that boy is never going to let you out of his sight for more than a few hours."

I looked up at them and felt only confusion, "But why? I mean we barely know each other, and we are completely different."

The others all looked at each other and shrugged, "listen sweetie, no one knows why anyone is attracted to someone else, but that doesn't make it any less real. Lord knows that someone like Jamal would not be my first pick but mmm." Esme said and the end of her sentiment made me question if she was talking about a man or a food item. The others all began to giggle, and I sat back thinking of the last few days with Gideon. After lunch we all headed back out to the shops. By the time we called for a cab we had enough bags to completely fill the trunk.

That night for dinner we had pot roast and corn bread. The conversation was light and there was a lot of laughter. I leaned into Gideon's now completely healed side, my head on his shoulder. He and Gwen thought it best to get the last session done early and now all he had was a shiny pink scar over his ribs.

"You ready to give the altar a try?" Randall asked softly from next to me as everyone else slowly finished eating, "If not we can still wait till tomorrow."

I took a deep breath and nodded. "We have to know what we have and what we don't," I looked at the faces around the table, "though I'd rather have as few people in there as possible. It's not an easy spell and I would rather have as few distractions as possible."

"By all means, go up alone, but do get going." Eris snarked and received an elbow in her side from Ade who was next to her. The two of them glared at each other.

"You will not be going alone," Gideon whispered to me. I smiled up at him and he brushed his lips over my forehead.

"Do you need an extra hand?" Zander asked.

I shook my head and stood with Gideon, "Just someone to show us where the supplies are."

"We can do that," Gwen said tilting her head toward Randall. With that we made our way back up the stairs with Randall and Gwen on our heels.

"What do you need?" Gwen asked as she made her way to the front of the group.

"Honestly if the altar is working correctly, I shouldn't need anything. If not, I'll need one chime in the colors of each Astral Plane, and black, white, blue and purple pillar candles, a bowl of salt, a bowl of water and an athame." I said racking my memory for what was used in the spell the previously at home. Had it really only been a week since I had been back on the ranch?

"We have all of those upstairs if needed" she said nodding. I followed her and Randall up the two sets of steps, Gideon at my side. When we got to the attic Gwen and Randall each moved to start searching through the boxes along the walls and Gideon stood behind me his hands on my shoulders.

"You ok?" he whispered against my hair.

I nodded, "I wasn't over exaggerating downstairs. This is the most complex spell I have ever done and it leaves you completely drained even if it doesn't work."

"Then if it doesn't work with just the Altar we will wait to try again with the supplies." Gwen said, her voice firm but kind.

Gideon turned me to look at him, "Is this dangerous?" his dark brown eyes searched mine, concern filling them.

I smiled as best I could, "Only if it works," I took his hands in mine, "As far as we know, without the Portals to act as anchors, if someone dies in the Astral Planes, then they are unable to wake here on the mortal Plane. They don't die, but they go into a sort of coma. None of us know if this is for sure the case, but it is what my parents warned me about when we were all first trying this spell."

"I don't like you doing this alone." He pulled me against him, his arms wrapping tightly around me.

"I know but we have to know if the Altar is working or not." I whispered against him, letting my own arms tighten around his waist. We stood like that for a moment before I stepped back, out of his arms and turned towards where the Altar sat in the center of the rug.

Taking a deep breath I stepped onto the rug and suppressed a shiver as the power of the runes washed over me. I knelt in front of the altar and ran my hands over the ancient wood. Closing my eyes, I dipped my fingers into the divots that once held the missing gemstones, but I felt no current of magic from the old table. Unlike what I could feel from the rug which pulsed and flowed around me, the Altar sat still and quiet under my hands. My stomach clenched. I placed both hands palm down on the edges of the table and took another deep breath. I reached out the same way I had back at the sanctuary back home, but there was nothing. I thought about the red haze of the first Plane, about the feel of working in the Plane, and again I reached for it in my mind. Still there was nothing. I let out a slow breath and let the chant slip from my lips in a soft whisper, "libera ferri, sphaerae, quaerere, ibi me accipere" Even with the words, there was no pull towards the Astral Planes.

"Guys, I think we will need the candles." I said softly.

I opened my eyes as Gideon joined me on the rug, arms laden with the supplies, "We will get this all set up but you aren't going to try it again tonight. You need your rest." I nodded and took them from him with a smile. I began placing them on the table, the small chimes resting almost perfectly within the divots of the missing gems. I placed the large pillars in the four corners as Gideon placed the bowl of salt and the bowl of water on either side of me, "Come on you, lets head downstairs and we can try this again tomorrow." I nodded and followed him down the stairs.

When we hit the first landing Eris stuck her head out of her bedroom. Gideon shook his head and glared at her, "Jeeze, did you even try?"

"Eris shut the hell up," I snapped, "You've done nothing but bitch since we got here. If you aren't going to help then keep your mouth shut." She huffed and slammed the door.

Gideon grinned down at me as we hit the second set of steps, "You know I think I like your feisty side."

"Oh you can shush up too." I grinned and poked his side.

"Hey careful there." He grinned. I rolled my eyes and poked his side again. He growled from next to me and suddenly I was pressed against the wall with his body pressed against mine.

I looked up at him and took a deep breath to try to slow my suddenly racing pulse, "What ya gonna do now?" I breathed.

He smirked down at me, "I am going to make you forget all that sass." He lowered his face towards mine and stopped with our lips only a breath from each other, "tell me no and I'll stop." His words were a warm breath. I couldn't seem to form words so instead lifted myself that miniscule distance and pressed my mouth to his. As soon as I closed that distance he took control again, pressing me back harder against the wall. One hand sliding to the small of my back to press me even firmer against his body, the other sliding into my hair, cradling my head. My hands slid up to rest on his chest, fingers curling into his shirt.

I let myself sink into the feel of him surrounding me. His lips on mine. His hands pressing me firmly against his body. I gasped as his lips slid from my lips to my jaw, "Gideon." His name came out breathy and I wasn't even sure why I was saying it. I heard him taking a hard deep breath and his head fell to my shoulder. I tucked my face against his neck and worked to catch my breath.

Slowly he pulled back, the hand from my hair sliding to my neck and the one from my back moving to take my hand. "I'm sorry Kenna." His voice was still harsh and breathy.

"For what?" I looked up at him confused.

"I let myself get carried away," he looked away from me.

I reached up and turned his face back to look at me, "Gideon, I closed the distance. You did nothing wrong." He smiled down at me and leaned down to press a softer, gentler kiss to my lips.

"Still want to go hang out with the others?" he asked.

I smiled up and nodded. He grinned and stepped back. We both headed down the stairs hand in hand.

"Any luck?" Ade asked as we joined her and several of the others in the front living room where they were just starting some new movie.

"No, we are going to try again tomorrow though." I reassured them even as Gideon pulled me down into his lap on the couch.

"We were talking," Esme said leaning forward, "What if we could find a way to tap into the ley lines? There are several that converge under the house and if we can learn to tap into them, maybe they can boost the spell you are using to help you use less of your energy."

I frowned thinking, "I have never worked with ley lines."

"My mom used to work with them, my grandma even more than she did," Misty said from where she was curled into an overstuffed chair, "I can talk to them about how to really tap into them."

"It's definitely something we could try." I leaned forward. I had never thought of tapping into the lay lines.

"Ok no more talk," Gideon pulled me back into his chest, "Time to relax and watch the movie." I laughed and settled back in his arms and turned to watch the movie.

I woke to Gideon's soft voice and him shaking my shoulders, "Time for bed darling." I stood and yawned stumbling towards the stairs. I felt his arm wrap around my waist and I leaned into his side as we made our way up the stairs. When we got to the room, Gideon left the lights off as we both changed into our pajamas. I crawled into the bed with another long yawn and let my head fall into the pillow nuzzling into it. I heard Gideon's soft chuckle, and then could feel the bed dip as he slipped in behind me. His arms wrapped around my waist and pulled me back against his chest, "Good night Kenna." He whispered into my hair. I wasn't sure if I answered or not before I let sleep wash over me again.

The next day we waited till after breakfast to go back up and try again to reach the Planes. Misty and Esme said they would work to find out how to hook into the ley lines just in case it didn't work. This time it was just Gideon and me who went up to the attic. As soon as we closed the door, I settled next to the Altar. Gideon knelt next to me as I lit the candles. When I held my hand out for the athame, instead of handing me the blade he took my hand and raised the palm to his mouth. He pressed his lips lightly to the center before lowering it again. His eyes never left mine as he drew the blade across my palm, pulling a gasp from me as my skin split easily. Leaning forward he pressed a kiss to my forehead before standing and leaving the circle. I let my blood drip into the mixed bowls, picturing my blood as a rope, stretchy but strong.

"libera ferri, sphaerae, quaerere, ibi me accipere" I chanted the words as I held my dripping hands over the two bowls and closed my eyes. I felt the tug just below my naval again and suddenly I felt like I was being jerked upward. I opened my eyes as I landed stumbling forward into the world shaded red. Again, I had made it to the first plane. Taking a quick look around to make sure I was alone I closed my eyes and repeated the words again, and again. There was no jerking motion and when I opened my eyes the world was still red. With a sigh of defeat, I let myself be pulled back to the mortal realm. I opened my eyes and looked up to the three people watching me and watched their faces blur with tears.

"I'm sorry, it didn't work, the altar is useless without the gems," I took a deep breath that shuddered out with a sob, "I failed you," I collapsed forward, "I failed them." I felt two strong arms pull me into a muscled chest and turned into Gideon, shaking as I felt the failure wash over me. Breath shuddering as my chest squeezed. I felt him pulling me close and his fingers stroking through my hair.

"We need to get Gwen to clean your hands." He said softly and I nodded unable to do much more.

CHAPTER 21

I LET HIM LEAD me from the Attic down the hall to the small room that Gwen had turned into her medical area. Gideon knocked softly before leading me inside.

"What's wrong?" Gwen asked her voice soft.

"Her hands." Gideon lifted my arms to show the two thin slices across the palms.

"They need to be cleaned and bound," Gwen ushered us in and closed to the door, immediately snapping into action.

Gideon sat in one of the chairs and pulled me into his lap, my back pressed against his chest, and held my hands out to Gwen. I looked up at them, "I'm sorry." My voice was a hoarse whisper.

"Whatever for?" Gwen asked, her brow furrowed.

"I failed, I didn't get the altar back whole."

"You didn't fail, you did your best and we will get the gems back Kenna," Gideon's voice was gruff. Suddenly it felt like fire washed over my palms and I gasped nearly jerking my hands back. I look down and saw a thick grey salve where the wounds once had been and looked up into Gwen's eyes, she smiled softly before wrapping my hands in gauze.

"Your hands will be fine in about twenty minutes," she said as she stood, "I'll leave you two alone." I watched her leave the room and let myself sink back into the safety of Gideon's arms.

"I don't know how to tell my parents," I whispered, "or what they will say when I do. They and the Goddess sent me out to retrieve the altar and return the ability to walk the astral planes and I failed."

"McKenna, look at me." I jerked my eyes up to meet his, the absolute command in his voice shocking me into action. He gripped my chin in his hands to hold me there, "You did not fail, you did everything you could. We will try again once we figure out the ley lines. If it still doesn't work then we will figure out something else. We will keep trying until we figure it out. And we will figure it out because you, darling, you are amazing. And if your parents can't see that then you don't need them."

"I won't have anywhere to go without them" I whispered shaking at the thought of never returning home again.

"You are a guardian now Kenna. You have a home here with the rest of us. And you can come home with me for visits. You can meet my parents and my older brother Matthew. They will love you just as much as I do,"

Leaning down he pressed his lips to mine, and I felt the breath leave my body. Pulling back he pressed his forehead to mine, "I know it's been only a short time Kenna, but I do love you. I will always love you and I will always take care of you." My chest tightened in shock and I looked up at him, love? "Let's go to our room, you need rest, you have tried this spell twice in as many days. I can see the drain it's had on you." I felt like I should have said something to him but I couldn't think. So I slid from his lap. We stood, and since my hands were bandaged Gideon wrapped his arm around my waist and pulled me into his side. He kissed the top of my head as we left the room.

"So, our room huh?" I asked grinning up at him when I could finally talk.

"I'm not letting you go sweetheart," he smirked down at me, "not now that I've found you" We made our way back up to the room and cuddled together on the bed. Gideon let his fingers play through my hair, my head resting on his chest. I wasn't sure how long we sat like that before I felt myself begin to drift off.

"Hey Gideon?"

"Yes Darling?"

"I love you too" I whispered as sleep pulled me in.

Gideon woke me for dinner a few hours later and we made our way downstairs to join the others.

"Gwen told us the bad news," Esme said as we walked in.

"I'm sorry guys, I tried, but it looks like without the gems the altar is useless."

"Hey don't give up on us yet. I called home today and talked to my mom and grandma. They said that our coven learned how to work with the ley lines from a pack of shifters." Misty said as she sat down across the table from me.

"I wish I would have asked Malek for his number," I roused and heard Gideon growl next to me. I ignored him.

"It would be nice to have a shifter to talk to that's for sure." Esme nodded.

"I can't argue with that, but I think that we can figure it out. I want to head into town tomorrow," Misty said as the guys began to laden the table with food at Gwen's direction, "I want to nudge some of the natives to see what they know about the local ley lines. From there I think we can start working on a spell to weave into the property, the house, and the rug upstairs to pull from the lines to strengthen things here."

"Why separate workings for grounds, house and rug? Why not just do one?" I asked as I pulled a piece of chicken onto my plate, ignoring Gideon as he continued to add second and third scoops of the sides to my plate.

"By doing multiple layers we can create a focus," Jamal said joining the conversation as he sat down next to Misty.

"Exactly," she stabbed her fork in his direction, "We start by making the grounds more powerful. This should not only help boost any magic we do on the grounds, but it should also make any herbs and spices we grow have a little bit more cosmic kick. This will also amp up any magic done in the house, since the house is on the grounds. We then add a second layer of amplification to the house. Again, making any magic worked with in the house more powerful, and adding an extra oomph to any potions, tinctures, amulets, pretty much anything we make in the house will have double the kick. We all know that all the artifacts will be placed in the attic, and we will need to make sure that the powers are able to reach all the covens, so we add a third amplification to the rug in the attic. We have the greatest amplification of power, in the place where our most complicated spells will be performed, and where our powers will be coming from."

"Well, let us know how we can help," I grinned at her.

"I will," She smiled back.

"Anyone not planning to join us on the trip into town tomorrow," Gwen said from near the other end of the table, "I am planning on getting the Garden out back started. Randall and Ed finished the first set of Garden beds and I received the seedlings I had been waiting on."

"I would be more than happy to stay behind and help," I smiled at her, "I miss working on the farm in the first Plane back home."

"I want to start laying runes around the property line and house," Jamal said, "With so much potential magic being loaded into one place we are going to need to make sure we are safe and also make it so that we aren't a magical beacon."

"That's a good idea," Alec nodded, "I think maybe a few small talismans with the wards worked in. We can put up some temporary ones for now and once Misty has the ley lines hooked in, we reward with stronger ones, both above and below ground."

"Good idea," Esme nodded, "we should probably look at getting a few metaphysical guardians for the house. I mean we have all seen what happened to the last guardians, and I don't know about the rest of you, but I would rather not die." The room was silent for a moment and most of us nodded in agreement.

Over the next few days I worked in the back yard with Gwen planting the dozen or more garden beds that had been built. I could feel the slight ache in my back and shoulders each night when we headed in to help the others with dinner. I could also feel the slow power build around us each day as the others began to call and direct the ley line powers and our natural powers to build the protections around the property line.

"I think tomorrow we can try to tap into the ley lines enough for you to try calling the powers." Misty said over dinner the second night.

"What do we do if it still doesn't work?" Eris asked.

"You will sit and whine while the rest of us figure out ways to fix things." I snapped at her. Not once had she stepped outside her comfort zone to help fortify the house and I was tired of her attitude.

"Listen, my coven does conjuring. What would you like me to conjure?" she snapped back.

"Well, if y'all are so good at conjuring then you can just conjure up the missing gemstones can't you? I mean why not just conjure all the missing artifacts."

"Kenna," Gideon's voice was soft.

"No Gideon. We have all been busting our butts to get things settled around here and to find the artifacts and she has done nothing to help," I turned back to the blonde, "You wanna know what you can do to help? Come get your manicured nails dirty and help me and Gwen in the garden, or help Alec and Jamal dig the pits for the protection talismans. Go out with Misty and Esme and learn how to work the ley lines and help them get those set up. If you can't manage to do any of that then get off your ass and clean or cook instead of acting like a spoiled little brat." I turned and left the room, my appetite suddenly gone.

"What the hell is your problem with me?" Eris's voice called after me as I walked out into the back yard.

I whirled around to face her, "I could ask you the same question. You have been doing nothing but picking at me since I walked in this door, yet you can't seem to actually do anything to help anyone."

I watched as she looked away, her eyes blinking rapidly. She was trying not to cry I realized, "no one wants me around, so I am just trying to stay out of everyone's way until I can find some semblance of a clue as to where the Triple Moon candle holder is." Her voice cracked slightly as she spoke.

"No one likes you Eris, because you make it so none of us want to. You want us to like you then be more likeable. I come from a large coven. Every day we all get up at dawn and we all work together to make things work. Some of us help to teach the children, some of us work the Planes, some of us keep the ranch running on the mortal Plane. It doesn't matter what we do, we help, and if we see someone else falling behind we don't become a bitch and treat them like shit, we help them. We are all going to be stuck together for a very long time Eris, I suggest you decide if you are ok being a complete outsider for the rest of your life or if you are going to stop pushing everyone in this house away."

"I'm sorry I've been such a bitch to you, but it was like since the moment you left the clearing you and Adriana were all anyone wanted to talk about."

"I doubt it was us. We just happen to be part of the first team to go looking for an artifact, and I bet, if you had actually listened to what they said it wasn't just me and Ade that they talked about," I sighed and took a deep breath. Eris had to be at least four years older than me but I felt like I was dealing with one of the pre-teens from back home, "You just aren't used to having to compete with guys are you? I bet back home your only competition was other girls because guys let you get your way. But here no one cares how pretty you are huh?"

"You get all that from the short time of us knowing each other?" I could see the resentment in her eyes.

"No Eris, I just happen to have known a lot of girls like you back home. Let me give you some advice, no one here wants to compete with you. We all want the same thing and we are all going to need to learn to work together if we are going to get the powers back."

"And because you say so everyone else will just fall into line." I could hear the resentment coming back into her voice.

"I don't have the energy to deal with you right now," I turned my back on her again and made my way over to the freshly filled garden beds. I pulled myself up and sat on the top board of one of them and looked up at the darkening sky. I could see the nearly full moon and let myself bask in the bright rays.

"Hey you ok?" I turned to find Ade, Esme, and Misty all coming out of the house, Eris was nowhere in sight.

"I'm tired. If what we try tomorrow doesn't work then I have no clue where to even begin looking for the missing gemstones."

"We will figure that out if this doesn't work," Ade said pulling herself up next to me, "You don't have to go through this alone you know."

"I know, but even with help I'm not sure what to do."

"Well to start, Esme and I want to help you tomorrow when you try to access the Planes." Misty said as she said on the ground a few feet in front of me.

"How? The spell doesn't work with anchors."

"We want to be conduits, not anchors," Esme said sitting on the other side of me, "We will hook into the ley lines and feed that power and energy into you, kind of like booster cables."

"It can't hurt to try," I smiled at them. We all sat in silence looking up at the darkening sky, "Gideon said he loves me." I let the words out in a whisper.

"This is a good thing," Esme said putting her arm around me.

"I've never even dated anyone, how am I supposed to know what love is?"

"You'll know," Misty smiled up at me.

The next day after an early dinner four of us made our way up to the attic. Esme and Misty so they could try to funnel the energy into me, Gideon, because he refused to stay away, and me. We replaced the candles and I sat in front of the Altar, Esme and Misty sat on either side of me. Gideon knelt across from me and again he drew the blade over first my palms and then theirs. When we locked hands I felt a swirl of power wrap around us, it lifted our hair to mingle with each other's, my bright red curls a stark contrast to their straight black hair. They both started whispering under their breath and I felt the magic intensify. I couldn't stop the gasp as I felt them begin to funnel the energy directly into me. Quickly I closed my eyes and began the incantation that had become so familiar. When I opened my eyes, everything was covered in the same red haze that I had become accustomed to but when I blinked, I could faintly make out an orange swirl beginning to fight with the red. I repeated the incantation and the orange of the second Plane grew stronger. Just as I began to repeat the incantation again I felt the hands in mine being pulled away and I fell back into myself. I looked up at Gideon ready to be angry, I could have made it to the next Plane. I knew I could.

"Look at them." He demanded softly. I turned to find them both slumped to their sides, blood trickling from their nose, eyes, and ears.

"Call Gwen," I scrambled to my knees and laid them on their backs. I began to immediately mop up the blood from Esme's face and there was as sudden flurry of activity. Gwen's voice was a calm in the storm. Quickly she had the other two moved into her room next door and followed on the heels of the men carrying them.

I knelt and watched as my two friends were carried away and a soft sob slipped from my lips. Gideon came over and wrapped his arms around me, holding me tight to him. "What do we do now?" I asked leaning into him as we walked towards the door, "I made it to two Planes, but I can't put anyone else in danger like I just did with the two of them." I turned and buried my face against his chest.

"We will figure something out. Maybe we need to create non-living conduits for the ley lines, or maybe whoever acts as conduits need their familiars near them. I don't know but we will figure it out, for now-"

"For now, you come down to talk to the Elf on the front steps" Randall cut in from halfway up the stairs.

Gideon looked down at me and our eyes met. Elves were one of the only other races that could walk the astral planes.

"Why is an Elf here?" I whispered to Gideon, wiping the tears from my face.

"I guess the only way we can find out is to go and talk to them," he replied. With a comforting squeeze around my waist, we followed Randall down the stairs to meet our new guest.

CHAPTER 22

THE LARGE FOYER SEEMED small even though there were only five people standing in it. The magic and tension were so thick it was as if we were suddenly under water. Standing in front of the door was a tall thin woman with skin as pale as moonlight and she had hair that hung in a straight white curtain to her lower back. She wore tight black leather pants with knee high leather boots and a zipped leather jacket. I could see the silver hilt of a knife sticking out of the top of one boot as she leaned against the door, arms crossed under her chest.

"You are the Shadow Walker." her voice slid over me and brought goosebumps to my skin as her velvet blue eyes bore into mine.

"I'm from the Shadow Witch Coven," I answered cautiously, "Who are you?" I asked as Jamal and Ed came down the stairs to stand at my back.

"You have reached the first plane," this was not a question, and she pushed away from the door with just her shoulders. I had to step in front of Gideon to keep him from blocking me from her.

"But we cannot reach the rest, the gemstones that hold our powers have been stolen. Can you help us?"

"Can we talk some place more private?" her gaze swept around the room.

"We are a single team here, anything you tell me they will also hear." I answered hoping I was saying the right thing.

She took a deep breath and tilted her head back and closed her eyes. She let out the breath slowly and lowered her eyes to mine, "I am ashamed to say that one of my kind joined with the dark witches and took the Gemstones from this plane. She was from another house and felt they needed to be returned to that from which they came. She felt the ability to walk the planes should be that of only the Elves. You should know, not all of us feel that way," she lifted a hand to stop the immediate protest from around the room, "the witches have been manipulating the planes for as long as the Elves. The witches had to solidify their powers into objects instead of keeping the abilities within themselves. We know they did this in order to lessen the likelihood of prosecution during the witch trials, which could have led to you losing the powers, possibly forever. To most of us that does not mean that the witches should lose their rights to the Astral Planes. Elves have never faced that kind of persecution and thus have never had to make that decision. Now I cannot go to the planes to retrieve your gems, that is not my power. What I can do is magnify your ability and help you reach all seven planes so that you can retrieve the gems."

"What is your name?" I asked again.

"Not here, again not all of my kind agree with me being here, and some will kill me if they find out that it was I who helped you. Now, was there a focus that the gems were placed in?"

"Yes, we have it upstairs." Gideon said.

"Then let us go upstairs."

"And why should we trust you?" Alec asked eyes narrowed in suspicion.

"Because without an Elf you do not have the ability to reach the planes and retrieve the Gems. Without the Gems you will never regain your ability to walk the planes." She turned to face him her eyes going cold, "you should trust me because I have nothing to gain by helping you and everything to lose, including my life."

"Kenna, we should discuss this, privately" Randall's voice was quiet behind me. I nodded and turned to head into the small living room off the foyer.

"We can keep an eye on our visitor," Zander said, he looked over to Alec who nodded.

The others all followed me into the small room and Jamal came in last, turning and holding his hands up along the door way. I could feel a soft pulse of magic before he dropped his hands and turned to face us.

"They won't be able to hear anything we say," he said turning back to face the rest of us.

"She is right. If the Gems are back in the Astral Planes, then she is also right about the fact that we need her help. The only other people who can reach the planes are the Elves," I looked at the others in the room, meeting Gideon's eyes last, "we need her, whether we trust her or not."

"You aren't going up there alone." his voice was firm, and I couldn't help but raise an eyebrow in challenge, "we have no proof that she can even do what she's saying she can. I understand that you feel you have to fix the Altar, but I won't let you act irresponsibly just for a chance."

"I agree with him Kenna," Randall said, "We need to proceed with more caution, especially after what happened with Esme and Misty. We know that we need to work to get all the artifacts back and online, but we have to do it smart. We can't be willing to die for something that may not work. Not only because no power is worth our lives but if we lose you before we get the gemstones back then we lose any hope of ever getting the Astral Planes back. Remember Kenna, you are the only one who can reach any of the Planes right now." I turned from them to look out the window, letting their words sink in and roll through my mind.

I took a deep breath and turned back to them, "I understand what you are saying, but we have been out of the Astral Planes for weeks now. This is the first hint we have gotten as to where the Gems went and how to retrieve them."

"Ok, so she told us where they are. Let's use that," Ed said from where he was leaning against the wall, "You can reach the first Plane right?"

I nodded, "Yeah, I can get to the first Plane no problem. It's an energy drain but I can do it."

"Then go to the first Plane, find the gem that's there. Come back and place the gem and we can open the first Plane to everyone. Maybe once the first Gems is in place you will be able to get to the second Plane and retrieve that Gem, so on and so on till we have all seven back."

I shook my head, "No, it will take too long. Not to mention that after we get the first one we have no guarantee that I will be able to get to the next Plane, and we have no way of preventing whoever this other Elf is from going and moving them. We have to get them all at once. I understand your concerns, but we have to at least try to do this with her help. She is only saying she will be boosting my natural abilities, if she can't do it then she can't and we can try to collect the Gems, one at a time. But even doing this one at a time, I will have to do it all in one day, we can't afford to waste time between."

"I have seen how drained you become from reaching the first Plane, there is no way you can go to all seven in one day," Gideon shook his head.

"Those are our only two options Gideon," I walked over and took his hands in mine, "I'm sorry, but we can't risk losing the Gemstones. If we can't get back to the Astral Planes, honestly no one knows what will happen."

"You aren't going to back down on this are you?" His eyes searched mine.

I smiled softly and shook my head, "I can't. This is what I have to do."

"You terrify me you know," he whispered pulling me against him and holding me tight.

"Says the one who jumped in front of a fireball." I whispered into his chest. I pulled back and turned in his arms to look at the others, "If anyone has any other ideas on how to do this, let me know, but this is the best thing I have heard since we found the Gems were gone." No one said anything so I stepped away from Gideon, "then let's go back and talk to our guest." The tension in the foyer was tangible when we came back in, "Zander what's going on?" I set my hand on the older gentleman's arm.

"Just don't trust her," his voice was just above a whisper.

"Well, we need to trust her," I looked past him to the Elf, "You say you can get us to all seven Astral Planes, how?"

"You already have the natural connection to the Planes; I will just be able to amplify your own abilities. I can only send you to all the

Planes Shadow Walker, no one else here has the ability t0 reach the first plain unassisted."

"She isn't going anywhere with you alone."

"Gideon," I set my hand on his arm.

"I will agree to allow five in the room with us. Four to uphold the elements, and one to place the gems onto the focus as they return to this plane. However, I do not have the ability to send anyone but the Shadow Walker into the Astral Planes, I myself do not even have the ability to travel there with her." she said looking between Gideon and me.

"Five will be more than enough," I said before anyone could object.

"Then please choose your protectors and let us move to where you have the focus so that we may get things moving."

"Gideon, Randall, Zander, Ade," I looked between Alec and Gwen, who had come down while we had been in the living room. Unable to decide I looked up at Gideon for his opinion.

"Alec," he nodded towards the former Marine, "and Gwen will be just outside the room with her healing kit in case something goes awry."

"I will agree to that." the Elf nodded.

"Ed, Jamal, Eris why don't you guys activate the protection wards around the property? I have a feeling that whatever we are about to do could use the extra security," Alec said with a nod toward the rancher.

"We can do that." Ed said with a nod. He led the others out the front door and Gwen headed upstairs to the small room that she had relabeled the infirmary. Randall turned and led the way up the stairs with the rest of us following closely behind, the Elf in the middle.

CHAPTER 23

ONCE INSIDE THE ATTIC I turned back to the Elf, "What is your name, please, I don't want to keep calling you, Elf."

"You can call me Morgana." she said. She began to slowly circle the rug and Altar, "is this the focus?"

"Yes, that's what the Gemstones were mounted in."

"It is beautiful craftsmanship. The Gems will lock back into place fairly easily. There is a residue of magic, so reactivating it will be no work at all."

"There is? I didn't feel anything."

She nodded, "It's very faint but it's there."

"Well, that's great news. First we need to know how to get them back." I said gently walking towards Morgana.

"Of course," she shook her head wearily as if coming out of a dream, "I can send you to the Astral Planes. All of them at once in a way. Once there you can retrieve the Gemstones that Nefesta has hidden there. To get them back to this Plane you must only get them close to their focal point, they will be drawn to it so let the stones guide you. I will place a charm circle around the focal point to strengthen the draw. Once they are within the perimeter of the tapestry here, they will appear on this Plane and Gideon can then place them on the Altar."

"All the Planes at once? How will that work?"

"Consciously you will only be in one, but your Astral Selves will be in all of them at once. You will need to start in the highest plane and work your way back to the lowest. Once you retrieve each Gem it will automatically pull you down to the next Plane, until you are back on this Plane."

I took a deep breath as I remembered my parents warning about what happens when one dies in the Astral Planes, "This Nefesta, is she dangerous?"

"All Elves are dangerous," Morgana's eyes flashed, "you would do well to remember that child."

I nodded in agreement, "Fine, you are all dangerous," My eyes darted over to Gideon then back to Morgana, "I was once told that if one dies in the Astral Planes that they are not able to come back to the mortal plane. Is that true?"

Morgana nodded solemnly, "That is a fact that none can change, if ones Astral Self is slain their mortal body will never wake again."

"Kenna this is too dangerous we will find another way," Gideon said turning me to face him.

"I will let you talk while I get the others ready," Morgana said softly.

"Gideon, there is no other way. We talked about this already, we must retrieve the stones or the Astral Planes will be lost to us forever." I looked up at him meeting his frantic gaze.

"Then let someone else do it." He pulled me against him, his arms a protective circle around me.

"There is no one else, love. I have to do this," I cupped his face in my hands. I lifted myself onto the tips of my toes to brush my lips over his, "I will be careful. But I must fulfill the destiny the Goddess has laid out for me," I whispered against his lips. I felt his arms tighten around my waist. He pulled me in against the strong line of his body, pressing his lips to mine. His hands were gentle but firm, one at the small of my back and one cupping the back of my head, both holding me to him as if he would never let me go.

When we were both breathless, he pulled back and rested his forehead on mine, "You have to come back to me Kenna."

"I will, promise," I closed my eyes and let myself get lost in his scent and the strength of his arms around me. I looked up at him, "You know, you could have a little faith in me."

"It's not you that makes me worry," he pressed a kiss to my forehead.

"Whenever you are ready, we will get started," Morgana's voice broke through our trance, "I have already instructed your fellow witches on how to start the circle of power."

We pulled back from each other and turned hand in hand to face the Elf. A pallet of blankets had been laid out next to the Altar. Randall, Zander, Ade, and Alec each stood in front of a large pillar candle, the flames flickering as their mouths moved in a silent chant.

"What do I do?" I asked my voice just over a whisper.

"As I said before I will help you into the seventh plane. Once there you just have to find the gemstones and return them here. Come lay next to the focus. The Gems and focus will call to each other so we want your body as close to the focus as we can as your astral self will be drawn to your body." I nodded, me and Gideon moved towards the Altar. I slowly lowered myself onto the blankets and laid back, one hand rested on my stomach. My other hand was in Gideon's as I stared up at the wood slatted ceiling, "I will need you to let go of each other before I can start," her voice was gentle. I felt my hand being raised and a light kiss was placed on the back of my hand before Gideon lowered it to my stomach with my other one and let go. I turned my head to look at him and was met with concerned brown eyes.

"I'll be back." I whispered smiling softly at him, "Keep an eye on Zipper for me, will you?" I asked as I saw the small bird flit in, followed closely by Onyx. Gideon nodded as both birds settled onto his shoulders.

"Are you ready Shadow Walker?" Taking a deep breath, I closed my eyes and nodded. I heard Morgana's melodic voice wash over me followed closely by a wave of magic. I felt myself being pulled from my body, my consciousness being stretched, and the sounds of the others fading away.

CHAPTER 24

I STUMBLED FORWARD GASPING for breath as I studied the purple haze that fogged the world. I shivered in the darker Plane and wished I had changed into something warmer before doing this. I could feel every hair on my body stand at attention and nearly jumped when I heard the scratching at the attic window before remembering the tree outside. I couldn't remember ever feeling so uncomfortable in any of the Planes before. I knelt next to the Altar and placed my hand on it. I traced the faint design until my finger dipped into one of the empty crevices and I felt a shock run up my arm to the top of my head. Morgana had been right. It was as if there was a string running from the crevice to wherever the Gem was hidden. I had managed to tap into the connection, and I felt as if I was being tugged away from the altar towards the Gem. I stood pulling my dagger from my boot as I did.

Call it a hunch, but I had a feeling Nefesta wouldn't leave the stone unprotected. I made my way from the house and shivered at the cool breeze that washed across my skin. I made my way down the empty streets of New Orleans following the tugging, pulling cord that ran through the top of my head. I wove my way through the French Quarter until I found myself in what seems to be a small magic shop. I wandered through the shelves of herbs and candles. I let my hands trace over the faint pulses from those that had already been infused with magic, empty spaces where I assumed those that were still mundane lay in the mortal realm. I looked through the cases of tarot cards and pendulums, an ever-growing wish list forming in my head, until I found myself at a counter lined in crystals. There amongst them was the first Gemstone. It was just about the size of my thumb nail and a perfect circular cut, the edges had been worn smooth over the years of soft touches. I quickly grabbed the stone and slipped it into my pocket. Turning from the counter I made my way back through the shelves toward the door.

I heard a deep rumbling growl and saw a shadow move on the other side of a shelf. Looking through the shelves I saw a large dark form, its back taller than my waist. I watched it crouch back and launch itself sideways at the shelf that was between us, knocking it over. I ran as the shelf began to fall toward me. I fell as the top of the shelf caught the back of my knees, its contents clattering to the floor. With a roar the beast launched itself onto the shelf. A gasp tore itself from my throat. It was a Dire Wolf, the Elven version of a Hell Hound. I slashed at it with my blade as I tried to wiggle out from under the shelf and it crawled up the shelves towards me. I could feel the edge of the shelf scraping into my legs through my jeans as I pulled my legs free.

I ran toward the door only to be slammed against it. I screamed as I felt the wolf's three-inch claws dig into my shoulders, slicing down my back. I pushed off the door turning and slamming the wolf into the wall eliciting a yelp from it. I ripped the door open and fled from the store. My shoes skidded on the sidewalk as I exited the building, teeth gritted from the pain in my shoulder.

Suddenly my back was on fire as the wolf slashed out with its claws, ripping my skin open once again. I screamed stabbing back blindly as I stumbled forward but continued to run. I felt resistance then a splash of wet heat along my hand. I had found my mark. I continued sprinting toward the house, each step agony as the torn muscles in my back and shoulder pulled. The gate at the front of the house was in sight when I was hit from behind yet again. I fell on all fours, then onto my stomach as I felt teeth sink into my shoulder and shake. I screamed and plunged the knife backward praying I would be lucky a second time. With a yelp and whine the beast fell off. I pulled myself to my feet and staggered through the gate. The purple hazed world swam in front of me and I tucked the bloodied blade into the back of my pants before pressing my free hand to the wounds at my throat. My lungs burned with every step and I stumbled up the stairs. Muscles protesting too much to stand I slowly climbed the four flights of stairs to the attic on my hands and knees. When the altar came into view, I felt the knot in my stomach release even as my sight started to fade. I fell to my side and pulled myself to the rug, the gemstone clutched in my hand.

"I'm sorry Gideon, I don't think I'll be coming back to you." I whispered the apology to the empty room as the hand holding the gem crossed over the edge of the rug and my vision faded.

I gasped sitting upright, blinking in confusion, into the blue hued world. I pressed my hands to my shoulder and then my back, both completely whole and undamaged. I stood slowly, but other than the feeling of danger that seemed to penetrate the air nothing was wrong.

"What in the Goddess is going on?" I muttered. I reached down and found my dagger back in my boot before scooting over to the Altar. I could see where one of the Gems had been placed back into its divot and traced my finger over it and to the next. Again, it felt as if a thread ran through my arm and out through my head. Standing, I hurried from the house but was wary of my surroundings as I left the grounds. This time I made my way in the opposite direction from where I had previously gone. After a few blocks I found myself standing in front of a gate to a graveyard and had to resist a shudder. I slowly pushed the gate open, wincing at the high-pitched squeak of the hinges, and nearly jumped when it slammed closed behind me. There was a blue fog that hid my feet from me as I walked down the alley like path between the raised tombs. I looked at them as I passed and wondered if the dark marks were real or if it was the effect of so much activity that showed only here in the Astral Planes. It looked like someone had painted with fire across the small stone buildings leaving scorch marks behind. I followed the tugging around corner after corner until I saw it. A glint in the fog. I rushed towards it, listening for any other sounds in the eerie graveyard.

In the center of a cross about two foot above my head was the gem mounted in the center. I climbed onto the small ledge of the tomb and standing on tiptoes and reaching up I used the tip of the dagger to pop the gem out of the concrete and caught it in my other hand. Immediately I heard a deep growl. I spun and pressed my back to the cold stone of the tomb. Between two of the small buildings there was a growing glow in the blue fog. As I watched the glow grew brighter, until the air burned. I watched the shadows and suddenly I could make out a large glowing figure. It was one of the fire jinn, an Ifrit. Gripping my dagger in one hand and the gem in the other I took a deep breath and pushed off the tomb. I sprinted through the fog back toward the gate. I used the edges of the tombs to pull myself around the corners, slowing as little as possible. When the gate appeared, I ran as fast as I could and jumped, opting to climb over instead of trying to open it again.

As my feet hit the sidewalk, I heard something heavy slam into the gate. I started to run faster. I only made it to the first corner when I felt a searing pain engulf my waist. Then I was airborne again and being hurled through the air. I felt the breath leave my body as I hit the cement and rolled. I heard cracking and felt my ribs give way under the hard ground. I rolled to all fours, tears streaming down my face. I felt the heat from the Ifrit as it landed in front of me. A grinning face masked in flames looked down at me when I lifted my gaze. My face was suddenly ablaze as he back handed me and sent me rolling into the street. I lay on the cold street panting as the winged demon stalked towards me.

I tightened my grip on my dagger, "Aqua Inaedifico," my voice a hoarse whisper. As he stepped over me, I pushed myself up with one palm on the cold cement and shoved the hand with the dagger up into him. The dagger, now completely encased in a thin membrane of water, slid under the Ifrits ribs and into his heart. With a roar of agony, the beast stumbled back and fell. He clutched at his chest as the flames that encased its body slowly receding starting at a point just above its heart.

Rolling to my knees I stumbled to my feet gasping as I felt the sharp cutting pain from inside my upper torso. One hand on the buildings that lined the streets, I made my way back to the house. By the time I reached the gate I was gritting my teeth in pain and sweat poured from my forehead. I leaned against the fence to catch my breath as my vision swam. Taking a few painful deep breaths, I opened the gate and made my way inside the house. Each stair to the attic sent electric shocks of pain ricocheting through my body. The burnt muscle and skin around my waist pulled and I was pretty sure at least one rib was broken. I was about halfway up the second flight when the toe of my shoe caught the edge of the stairs and sent me pitching forward.

A scream tore from my lips as I felt a sharp piercing pain in my chest. As I tried to push myself back to my feet, I couldn't suppress a cough and was surprised to see a wet splatter of blood marking the stairs. My rib must have punctured my lung. I slowly started my way up the stairs again, each one increasingly more difficult and painful. Several times my hands and knees slipped on blood on the stairs. The blood that was dripping from my mouth and bubbling from my nose slid down my face with each breath. Finally, I slumped against the Altar and let the Gem roll from my hands. I had five more to retrieve, but I knew now that there was no way I was ever going to wake up from this and see my love again.

I sat up and the world was ablaze in red. I stood and walked to the cabinet in the wall opening it. Removing the long thin sword, I had previously discovered there, I walked back to the Altar. This was it, the last and final gem. After this my people would have the ability to walk the planes again. My only hope was that they would never see any of my former selves here. Dire Wolves, Ifrits, Pixies, explosions, I had never known one could produce so many protections on the Astral Planes. I touched the only remaining space in the Altar and felt the sharp tug run up my arm and through my lower abdomen, just above the apex of my legs. I walked briskly from the house; the sword held loose but ready at my side. As with the other six times I had walked from the house, the direction I was pulled in was different. This time I found myself entering a church at the very heart of New Orleans, and this time I wasn't alone. There standing at the churches altar in the sanctuary was an elf.

Like Morgana she stood tall and proud, back straight. Her hair was pulled back in a high ponytail yet it still reached her lower back in a wavy mass of black. When she turned to face me, her eyes were the colors of the ocean, a bright teal color. She was gorgeous but there was a glint in her eyes that made her cold and ugly.

"Nesfta, give me the gem of my ancestors." I demanded, tightening my hold on the sword.

"You and your kind are not worthy of walking these planes" she hissed turning to face me. I saw the glint of the Gem behind her on the altar and slowly advanced. She snapped her fingers and a long thin blade like my own appeared in her hand, "if you want the stone you will have to come and get it little witch."

I narrowed my eyes. I lifted my blade into both hands, just as I brought it up in front of me, she rushed me. I had just enough time to block her and she was gone again, faster than I could see. Again, and again she came at me. Forcing me to block and defend, she was faster than anything I had ever seen before. Each time I swung my blade where she was, she would then be feet away laughing. I watched her come at me again but this time when I went to block her, she wasn't there and there was a throbbing pain in my stomach. I looked down to see her sword protruding from me and my breath caught in my throat. I fell to my knees as she let go of the blade and fell back onto my heels as she walked around to face me, grinning down smugly.

She leaned in until our noses nearly touched, "and you were so close, only the final one left and you failed."

"I haven't failed yet" I gritted out, the pain already starting to numb my body in the now oh so familiar way.

"You are dying Shadow Walker, I am alive to keep you from the stone,"

"One thing Nestfa, when going for the kill, you should make it faster next time," I advised before shoving my dagger into her throat under her jaw and up through her mouth. I watched as her eyes rolled back and the life left her body as she fell in a heap in front of me. Gripping the blade of her sword I scream as I slowly started to push it back out of me. Once free of the metal blade I staggered to the altar and grabbed the Gemstone before ripping the long altar cloth off. Tearing it into strips I wrapped it repeatedly around my abdomen to stem the blood flow. I stepped around the Elf's body and staggered from the church.

By the time I made it to the house the cloth around my waist had bled through and I could feel myself growing cold. Death by slow blood loss sucks. I pulled myself up the stairs and to crawl my way to the Altar, fingers fumbling as I pushed the gem into the final slot.

CHAPTER 25

GIDEONS POV

Morgana knelt next to Kenna and held her hands out over her body. She spoke softly, her words like a song. I could feel power building, much like I had when Esme and Misty had tried to help Kenna earlier that day. I moved around to the other side of the Altar, wondering if this was putting as much strain on the elf as it had them, but her face was peaceful. I watched Kenna's chest lift slightly from the pile of blankets before it relaxed back down again and Morgana sat back on her heels.

"She's there."

"Now what?" I demanded as Zipper took flight and circled his owner before settling on her chest just above her heart.

"Now we wait for the Gems to begin to appear and then for her to wake." I caught Randall's gaze and he flicked it towards the door. I wanted to argue, I didn't want to leave Kenna's side, but I knew he was right. We needed to keep Gwen informed of what was happening so she could keep the others outside up to date. I strode over to the door cracking it open enough to see Gwen sitting on a small stool in the hallway, a bowl of herbs in her lap.

"She's in," I said softly, "how are the others?"

"They are asleep for now," she looked up and her eyes helped to calm me, "Go be with your love Gideon. I will knock if anything changes." I nodded and closed the door. I moved back and sat next to Kenna, taking her hand in mine as I leaned back against the Altar.

I watched Kenna's body bow off the pallet and toss from side to side again before falling limp and still once again. Zipper hadn't woken again after her initial convulsion, and I had laid the small bird near her. I didn't like that she seemed to be in pain repeatedly, and I liked even less that her Familiar was no longer responding to anything.

"Something is going wrong." I repeated for what felt like the hundredth time and looked up at Morgana. Three of the seven stones had appeared at several locations around the rug and Altar. I had moved each of them into their place. Just then the fourth rolled across the floor and stopped inches from my feet. I slid the gem over the Altar until it pulsed with a faint light and slid it into the groove. Turning back to Kenna I ran my palm over her soft cheek and leaned down to press my lips to her forehead. I hoped that she was still safe even as my gut clenched in fear. "You have to send me in to help her" I looked back up to the dark haired elf.

"I can't," she shook her head, "I'm sorry but that is not my gift. I can't manipulate the planes."

"Then how did you get her in there" I growled standing and walked till I stood toe to toe with the Elf staring down at her.

"I told you before, I can manipulate other's powers. I was able to magnify her already natural ability to walk to the first plane without the gemstones so that she could reach all of them. If anyone else here had the ability I could send them in after her but you don't. You won't be able to reach the Astral Planes until she has retrieved the last Gemstone. I am sorry but there is nothing that I can do."

"Something keeps hurting her. She shouldn't be doing this alone," I turned back to face Kenna. I ran my hand through my hair and gave the strands a soft tug, "I should be in there with her. I should be helping her, protecting her." I knelt next to Kenna's body and ran my hand over her soft red curls. My heart clenched at the thought of her green eyes never sparkling in laughter again. It was already something they didn't do nearly enough. Her body jerked, face twisting into pain, "Shh baby, I'm here. I'm here and I'm not going anywhere. You aren't alone. I believe in you, you can do this and you will come back to me." her body slumped, limp again, and another gem rolled into existence. I pressed a kiss to her forehead before I stood and picked up the small stone to return it to its place on the Altar. I sat back down next to her and pulled her head into my lap. I soothed my hand over her hair repeatedly and prayed to the Goddess and the moon and anyone else that would listen that she would soon be opening her eyes, smiling up at me.

CHAPTER 26

IT SEEMED LIKE AN eternity later when the final stone appeared. This time directly into the remaining slot. I looked down urging Kenna to open her eyes, but she didn't.

"Hold your hands over the Altar and chant 'libera ferri, sphaerae, quaerere, ibi me accipere," The Elf urged from where she stood outside of the circle. I rushed over and knelt next to the Altar and held my hand over it palms down. I could feel a warmth pulling at me before I even started the chant.

"Libera ferri, sphaerae, quarerere, ibi me accipere" as soon as the last word left my lips the world spun around me. Colors blurred into one another until I knelt in the same world, and not. I could still see Randall, Zander, Ade, and Alec where they stood at their candles, hands out and to the side but they were blurred and distant. The world swam in swirls of colors and there around me I saw Kenna.

She lay at my feet dead. I could see six forms of her in six pools of blood that had poured from the wounds on her body. And there slumped over the Altar she lay again, body swirling in pulses of red, her back rising the smallest bit. I rushed over and pulled her into my arms. Her midsection was wrapped in a thick cloth with blood seeping slowly through.

"Kenna, baby open your eyes" her face blurred, and I blinked away the tears. Her lashes fluttered and my heart caught at the dullness that filled her once lively eyes.

"Gideon?" her voice was a hoarse breath.

"I'm here baby," I pulled her to my chest and rocked her. I felt her fingers twisting in my shirt and I rested my cheek atop her head, "I've got you; I am so sorry you were alone but I'm here now. I came as soon as I could Kenna." Time seemed to pause around us or maybe it was that I stopped caring. My throat and chest ached as her hand slowly grew limp against my chest. By the time I lifted my cheek from hers, she had grown cold in my arms. Slowly I stood lifting Kenna in my arms. I carried her down the stairs to the room we had shared and laid her on the bed. I went back to the attic and lifted another of her Astral selves into my arms and carried them down to the room as well. One by one I carried each of Kenna's Astral selves to our room and laid them on the bed, watching as they each melded into one another. Their colors swirling together but never mixing. The wounds on each super imposing over the others so that by the time all seven lay together there wasn't one place that was left unbloodied or burned. I walked back to the attic one last time and closed my eyes wishing to be back on the mortal plane.

My eyes opened and I slumped over the Altar. The seven gems winked at me tauntingly. They were gleaming in the light from the four flames like seven droplets of blood. They were what Kenna had given her life for repeatedly and in what appeared to be painful ways. I slammed my fists onto the old wood and swore as I felt the sides bruise instantly as the wood creaked.

"Where is Kenna?" Ade asked breaking her chant for the first time in nearly six hours. As soon as she did her candle faltered and died the smoke swirling to the ceiling.

I looked up and met her dark concerned eyes, all I could do was shake my head. I looked around and watched as the other three candles extinguished as their keepers also stopped their chants. Their charge was gone. That was when I noticed that the elf was gone.

"Where is she?" my words a growl as I stood.

"She left as soon as you slipped into the astral plane, she said her job here was finished." Alec said in his gruff voice.

"She knew. She knew as soon as Kenna didn't wake up and she didn't want to be here to face you," Zander's voice was full of malice.

I looked at Randall, "Get Gwen, I need her now."

The old biker only nodded as he left the room and returned only seconds later with Gwen at his side. With no explanation I took her hand in mine and repeated the words the Elf had given me. The same words that I had once heard Kenna herself say in a voice filled with hope and as much desperation as I felt now. The world swirled around us and I felt Gwen falter next to me. I slipped an arm around her waist to steady her.

Once she was steady again, I quickly led her down to the room where Kenna laid mangled on the bed, "Heal her, please," my voice caught as I turned to face Gwen.

"I'm sorry Gideon but I can't. Maybe if I had been there with her. Maybe then I could have healed some of these wounds and saved her," her eyes filled with tears as she looked down at Kenna. She ran a hand over her curls, "But even I cannot heal the dead Gideon," she looked up at me and I saw sorrow and apology in her eyes.

I nodded once, and closed my eyes forcing myself to swallow past the lump that was forming in my throat. We walked side by side back to the attic in silence and in silence we returned to the mortal plane. I walked over and placed Zipper's still form on Kenna's still chest before I lifted her from the blankets and into my arms. I cradled her to my chest like I had in the red filled world and stood.

"Gideon," Randall called after me.

"Leave him to grieve his love," Gwen's voice softly admonished.

I carried her down to our room, now the eighth time I had done so, and again laid her in our bed. This time though, she lay on the bed still as the dead minus the barely there rise and fall of her chest, not an imperfection to be found on her near porcelain skin. I fell to my knees as a sob ripped through my chest. I felt as though some enormous fist was clenching inside of me, pulling and tearing at my heart. I slumped forward, an arm on either side of her, my face buried in her stomach. There I cried for the first time that I could remember since I was a small boy. The happiness that had only just started inside of me began to slowly fade back into non-existence. As it did, I let myself fade into the blackness of unconsciousness.

CHAPTER 27

WHEN I FINALLY LIFTED my head again the light outside of the windows had come and was darkening again. I slowly stood, my body protesting the movement after being still for so long. I scrubbed my hands over my face before I looked down at Kenna one more time. I pulled the blanket up and over her, covering her completely, laying one last gentle kiss to her forehead. I walked over to her bag and rummaged through until I found the barely used cellphone. I turned it on and quickly pulled up the only number Kenna had called since we had met. With my back still to the bed I dialed the number. It rang three times before it was answered. The female voice that answered the call made my knees go weak with how close to Kenna's it sounded.

"Kenna darling, I knew you could do it," she said excitedly.

"I'm so sorry." I looked up to the ceiling and blinked, "this is Gideon. You don't know me, but I'm a friend of Kenna's."

"Where is McKenna?" the distrust in the voice made me smile, I was seeing where she got her attitude from.

"Ma'am, McKenna went into the Astral Planes yesterday with the help of an elf. She was able to retrieve the gems for the Altar," I looked back at the still form under the blanket. I had to take a slow breath, "She did her best but she didn't make it out."

"Oh God" the words were breathy, "My baby."

"I am so sorry ma'am," I hung up the phone before I could hear her mother break down. I couldn't bear hearing a voice that sounded so like Kenna's in so much pain. I turned the phone off and set it on the dresser. I grabbed my bag from the corner and lifted it onto my shoulder before walking out of the room. I closed the door and laid my hand on the wood. I quickly sealed and protected the room from everyone but me. I paused feeling an edge of power on the door, someone had blessed the door while I had been inside. I walked down the stairs and was shocked to see that the house had been dressed in mourning black.

"Gideon?" Gwen's soft voice called from the small parlor off the entry way.

I walked in and looked around at the now familiar faces of friends and acquaintances. A second look around confirmed there were a few missing, "Where are Zander, Randall, Alec and Ed?" I asked Gwen.

"They left this morning to go look for the mirror." Eris said softly.

"Good, we will need all of the artifacts if we are going to bring Kenna back."

"Oh Gideon," Gwen's voice was gentle but patronizing, "Kenna is gone, there is no saving her."

"No," I closed my eyes and breathed deeply to calm myself when most of the others in the room jumped at my word, "No. We will not give up on her. Once we have all of our abilities back, then we can save her. We will save her," I opened my eyes and looked around at the others, "I will bring her back. Back to her family and back to me."

"How?" Misty asked form where she was curled up on the couch, "From what the others said, the Elf said once you die in the Astral Planes you die."

I looked at them all, "At full power we can control time and manipulate the energy around us. We are Masters of Illusion and Visibility. We talk to the dead and conjure things at will. We can move things with a thought and heal even the worst wounds. We can move from place to place in the blink of an eye, see the future and we can walk the Planes freely. So, we will get the artifacts back, we will master them, and we will bring Kenna back."

ACKNOWLEDGMENTS

I want to thank my best friend Stephanie, my grandma and my aunt. All of whome this book would not have been possible. A thank you to the rest of my family who have put up with my crazy schedule over the last two years. And finally to my writers group who encouraged me from the beginning.

ABOUT AUTHOR

Ana Michelle was raised in Southeastern Wisconsin, with two
younger siblings. Reading books was the best way to get through the winters
there. Ana started writing in the sixth grade as her escape during summer
vacations. Since the first time she sat down with a computer to type her first
story, her aspiration was to be a writer. Garnet Fire is her debut novel and
the first book in the Gemstone Witch Series.

CPSIA information can be obtained
at www.ICGtesting.com
Printed in the USA
JSHW022217210822
29505JS00003B/13

9 781639 580019